My Name is Sherlock Holmes

My Name is Sherlock Holmes

Narrated by John H. Watson MD

LUTE PUBLISHING

First published in 2015

ISBN 978-0-9931453-0-8

Typeset by Deltatype Ltd, Birkenhead, Merseyside
Printed and bound by CPI Group (UK) Ltd,
Croydon, CRO 4YY

for Lute Publishing

'There is nothing more deceptive than an obvious fact'

Sherlock Holmes

Contents

The First Cases

When engaged in his work, Sherlock Holmes is for the most part extremely active and energetic, unlike his brother Mycroft. He once said to me, 'If the art of the detective began and ended in reasoning from an arm-chair, my brother would be the greatest criminal agent that ever lived. But he has no ambition and no energy.' In this respect, Holmes has the edge. But there was a time when I first met Holmes that his work was largely confined to the four walls of our sitting-room; clients would call, present their problem, and he would make his comments. He would pocket his fee and they would leave. These cases were remarkable not so much for their sensationalism, but rather more for their logic; in that respect, they reigned supreme over many of his famous cases and it is of a few of these cases that I now wish to relate.

It was in the spring of 1881 that Holmes and I were in the sitting-room after breakfast, whereupon Holmes said that he might expect a number of callers that morning, as he often did. It had surprised me to find that he had a great number of acquaintances. He had finally told me who these acquaintances were and what his business with them was; that he was a 'consulting detective', the only one in London, and that they were his clients. I immediately offered to leave the room, as I always did on these occasions. However, on this particular morning, he asked me to stay.

"I would welcome a side-kick of sorts," said Holmes. "You have proven yourself to be discreet and trustworthy, and as a doctor, you will know how to interact with clients. Perhaps you might even be so good as to take notes."

"Why, certainly, Holmes," I said. I was still in a convalescent state but the prospect of this light work did not repel me. "It is obvious to me that your clients will require confidentiality when laying out their problems before you. I shall be the soul of discretion."

"Then you are the very man for me," said Holmes. "The first is due at ten o'clock. A young lady recently married to a banker, now living in Knightsbridge."

Mrs. Hudson came in to collect the breakfast dishes. "There is a young lady across the street who keeps looking at her watch and up at our windows," she said. "I believe she has an appointment."

"Well, we shall not disturb her," said Holmes. "It is three minutes to ten. She will ring at ten o'clock precisely, I'll warrant."

"She must fear terribly of being too late or too early," I said. The clock on the mantelpiece ticked on until the minute hand reached its highest point. At this moment, the bell downstairs rang out. Moments later, the client was shown in, introduced as Mrs. Ella Wellesley.

The lady who had entered the sitting-room was smartly dressed in a mutton sleeve blouse, black tie and black skirt. She did them justice and they her. Unlike many of the clients that Holmes received at this time, this woman had not been sent round by a private inquiry agency but had come on her own initiative. Despite her neat apparel, she had a vague, absent-minded expression, as though she lived most of her life in another world. However, on seeing Holmes, her expression became alert and concentrated. He motioned her to sit in the armchair that was designated as the 'client's chair' and sat down opposite.

"Please lay the problem before me," he said, patiently.

"I have come about a missing key," she said, at once. "The key to my jewellery box. I mislaid it about six months ago."

"Is the jewellery box still in your possession?" enquired Holmes.

"Yes and no. My husband confiscated it shortly after we were married. He said it gave me too much independence. He placed it in a drawer in his study where it still is; at least, it was there this morning."

"Why do you not simply force it open?"

"The box is legally my husband's property. It has been, since I married him. If I were to do that he would be sure to realize it."

"If the box is now your husband's property, what do you hope to achieve by opening it?"

"I wish to remove my diamonds. My husband does not know what is in the box. When he confiscated it he asked me for the key. I told him that I had lost it, which was true."

"If you were to remove the diamonds, the box would become lighter. Your husband would know that something had been taken out of it."

"He would not notice. If I could just get my diamonds, I would no longer feel trapped, as I do now. It is the only piece of jewellery that I own of any real value. All the others are just trinkets, worth no more than a few hundred pounds."

"This whole enterprise may soon become unnecessary," said Holmes. "The Married Women's Property Act has been proposed and may be passed within the year. Your jewellery will then become yours again and you will be free to do as you like."

Mrs. Wellesley appeared depressed.

"That Act will not be passed in my lifetime," she said. "Nobody wants it, apart from me and a few other women. Most married women have no property of their own, and so it would be of no advantage to them."

"That is true," said Holmes. "However, the few women, and indeed, the few men who do want it have been extremely aggressive in their action to get this law passed. We are approaching a period of rapid change."

"Well, in any case, that does not help me now," said the lady.

"All right," said Holmes. "Then tell me, before you lost the key, where did you normally keep it?"

"I did not normally keep it anywhere in particular," said the lady. "I might leave it on the dressing table, in the drawer, in the bathroom, on the window sill, or anywhere, really."

"That is most inadvisable," said Holmes. "It is the reason why you lost the key. If the key is recovered, I suggest that you designate a place for it, and whenever it is not in use, you return it to that place."

"Yes, I know," said the lady. "But it is so uncreative to

be that organized. However, if I find it, I will not wish to lose it again. Please help me to find it."

Holmes placed his fingertips together in an arch and closed his eyes.

"Cast your mind back to the last time that you remember seeing the key," he began.

"Well," said the lady. "It was a few nights after we were married. I was sitting at the dressing-table in my bedchamber (I have my own room. I insisted upon that proviso before we married). I remember opening the jewellery box and examining my jewellery; then I closed the box and locked it with the key. That is all I remember."

"What did you do with the key after you had locked the box?" asked Holmes.

"I can't remember."

"I presume you have looked 'everywhere'."

"Yes, Mr. Holmes. I have spent days searching for it."

"And not found it."

"Yes."

"Then clearly, you have not looked everywhere."

"No, but I cannot think where else to look."

Holmes opened his eyes again. "You have two options available to you," he said. "One: go over the room in which you last saw the key inch by inch in a systematic manner. Two: reconstruct the scenario of when you last saw the key."

"I have already performed the first option," said the young lady.

"I suspect that your search was not systematic. However, you cannot do that here. Unlike the second option." He paused, as though considering something. "Let us assume that this writing desk is your dressing table," he said, going over to this piece of furniture. He pulled out the chair in front of it. "If you would be so good as to sit down here."

Ella Wellesley glided over to the desk and sat dutifully down.

"Now," said Holmes. "Let us pretend that this box is your jewellery box." He produced a small wooden box and placed it in front of his client.

"And this is the key. You will now go through the motions of what you did on that fateful evening when you last saw the key. Wait! What were you wearing on that occasion?"

"My negligee, nightdress and slippers."

"Alas, we have no negligee on the premises. However, Mrs. Hudson may be able to avail." He went over to the door and opened it.

"Mrs. Hudson!" he called out, in the slightly irritated tone that our poor landlady was now accustomed to.

Mrs. Hudson appeared in no short time.

"Yes, sir?" she asked.

"You wouldn't happen to have a negligee lying around, would you? And some slippers?"

"I do," said Mrs. Hudson. "Would you like me to bring them up?"

"Yes," said Holmes. Mrs. Hudson disappeared again.

"When Mrs. Hudson returns, would you be so good as to don the negligee and slippers that she is so kindly providing for this experiment?" said Holmes. "I am aware that it is a little irregular, but it may help immensely in the finding of your key."

"All right," said Ella Wellesley. It was within minutes that the young lady was sitting at the writing desk in front of the wooden box, an oddly well-fitting lace negligee worn over her clothes, and satin slippers on her feet. Holmes returned to his armchair.

"Now," he said. "Let us begin. Perform the actions that you did on that evening, stating them out loud as you do so."

Ella Wellesley picked up the key to the wooden box. "I unlocked my jewellery box," she said, unlocking the wooden box. "I opened the box. I picked up my diamond necklace and held it up to the light. I remember thinking, why did I need to get married at all, when I had this necklace. It would have supported a modest life for twenty years. I then returned it to its place in the box. I closed the box and locked it. I must have, for it was locked when my husband confiscated it."

Holmes said nothing. I too, remained silent.

"At this point, my memory becomes hazy," said Ella Wellesley. "I may have put the key in my pocket. Yes, I think I could have. I went to the bathroom and to the lavatory." She stood up and walked over to the door to our own bathroom. "Then, I removed my negligee and hung it over the end of the bed." Ella Wellesley removed the borrowed negligee and laid it over an armchair. The key immediately fell to the floor. "I then went to bed, removing my slippers just before I did so."

"And that was the last you saw of the key?"

"Yes," said Ella Wellesley. "Only it could not have fallen to the floor; I looked all over the floor, including under the bed."

"Are you sure that you placed your negligee over the end of the bed so that the lower part of it was draped over the outside?" asked Holmes.

"No," said Ella Wellesley. "I may have hung it the other way round."

"Then let us try again," said Holmes, picking up the key and handing it to Ella Wellesley. She returned to the writing desk, clad in the negligee once more and with the key in its pocket. Again, she went to the armchair and placed the negligee over the edge of the chair again; this time the key fell out and dropped behind the chair cushion.

Ella Wellesley stared. "I believe I now know what happened to my key," she said. "It has slipped down between the end of the bed and the mattress."

"If you would be so good as to ascertain this," said Holmes. "If the key is not there, do not hesitate to return and I will delve more deeply into the matter."

"I would be surprised if it were not there," said she. "Why in six whole months, did I not think of that? I am most indebted to you, Mr. Holmes." The lady swung out of the room.

"You have a way with women, despite your deplorable views about them," I commented, after the swish of her skirts was followed by the slamming of the door. However, this did not prompt a discussion on the subject. "When are you expecting the next client?" I asked in order to break the silence that followed.

"I am always expecting clients," said Holmes. "They know where to find me, thanks to my growing reputation."

I stepped over to the broad windows that illuminated the room. "I believe there is one coming now," I said, observing a young man in a top hat, with a cool manner, moustache and cane, approaching our front door. "He appears to be fairly well-heeled. I wonder what he can want."

"He may require our absolute discretion," said Holmes. "However, I insist that you remain, even if he objects."

"If you think so, Holmes," I said, sitting down again.

An even tread ascended the steps to the first floor landing, preceded by those of Billy. Moments later, the door to the sitting room opened.

"I am Luigi Antonio," said the swarthy gentleman who stood before us, with slick, glossy hair and attired in a dark suit of an elegant cut. "I have heard that you are a detective of the highest class, whose discretion is absolute." He seemed a lot more pleased to see Holmes than he did me. However, he did not comment.

"You have heard correctly," said Holmes. "If you would be so good as to sit down."

Luigi Antonio immediately obliged, placing a well-brushed top hat upon the table beside him. "Do you mind if I smoke?" he asked, producing a silver cigarette case.

"Not at all," said Holmes.

The dapper, young man opened the case and offered it to Holmes. "No, thank you," said Holmes. "I never smoke in the presence of clients."

As in an afterthought, the gentleman then offered me the case as well, but I politely refused. He then took out a cigarette himself and lit it with a fancy lighter.

"You spent your childhood in Italy," said Holmes. "And have recently been to the opera. Your wife is an accomplished pianist."

"I have heard of your peculiar talent for deducing such things," said the gentleman. "And must confess my curiosity as to how you could know. My appearance is indeed that of an Italian, and English is my second language. However, I was under the impression that I had no accent."

"You do not," said Holmes. "However, your manner is Italian. When you entered this room, you bowed smilingly at me. Only in France and Italy is this done. In Spain and the East, a man bows gravely. This indicates that at least your childhood was spent in Italy, if not your adulthood; however, your bilingualism suggests that you arrived here at a fairly early age."

"Quite so," said Luigi Antonio. "As for your last statement, that my wife is an accomplished pianist, I am less bemused. Although not on the level of a concert pianist, she has been known to play in churches around London at lunchtime. She shares my surname. But what made you so sure that she was my wife?"

"When you held out your cigarette case to me, I observed for an instant the name 'Carlotta' inscribed on your cufflink. As the name of the pianist who played at St. George's church last Thursday was Carlotta Antonio, it is beyond coincidence that she is not your wife."

"Very good, Mr. Holmes," said Luigi Antonio. "And how did you know that I had been to the opera recently?"

"That is so embarrassingly obvious that I hesitate to say it," said Holmes. "As you placed you top hat upon the table, I could not help but notice a cloakroom ticket, pinned to its inside. Only at the Royal Italian Opera, Covent Garden, are tickets of that style and colour used."

"Perhaps you can also work out why I am here," said the Italian.

"That would be sheer guesswork. I never guess," said Holmes. "Pray enlighten me."

The Italian gentleman drew on his cigarette and looked discontentedly around the room. "My wife is has a lover," he said, finally.

"I am very sorry to hear it. What is it that you wish me to do?" asked Holmes.

"I wish you to confirm my suspicions."

"So they are merely suspicions. You have no proof."

"No."

"If you were to acquire the proof, what would you do with it?"

"Do? Nothing. It is not divorce that I am after, Mr. Holmes," said Luigi Antonio. "It was a marriage of love; at least, on my part."

"But you think, not on hers."

The man sighed heavily. "I do not know," he said. "I have never asked her."

"Why do you believe that she has a lover?" enquired Holmes.

"She has on one occasion gone out in the afternoon, to an hotel. My valet established this. She tells me of all of her excursions but did not of this one."

"Is that all?"

"No. Once, I entered her bed chamber without knocking. She was holding a letter which she instantly hid behind her back as soon as I entered the room."

"Did you ask her who the letter was from?"

"No. It did not seem appropriate."

"And these two events are your sole evidence."

"Yes. It is enough for me. One of these events on its own, perhaps not. But together …I am paying for my ambition in love, Mr. Holmes. She is intellectually my superior."

"Have you confronted her concerning your fears?"

"No. I thought it better to investigate without her knowledge."

"I doubt if she would appreciate it, if she knew."

"Yes, but she does not know."

There was a pause in which Holmes appeared to be consulting himself.

"Your hypothesis holds no contradiction to the facts," he said, eventually. "However, a lack of contradiction is not proof. There are, no doubt, a whole string of hypotheses that would fit those very same facts. Let us take the first piece of evidence: that your wife is known to have visited a London hotel one afternoon. I shall list some of the possible reasons for this. One: she is a typewriter and was called to the hotel to type some material."

"She owns no typewriting machine."

"Then we may all but eliminate that possibility. Two: she has a position as piano player in the tea room."

"My wife is incapable of playing lounge music," said Mr. Antonio. "Her repertoire consists solely of Baroque. She has a distaste for anything else."

"In that case, that possibility is also very unlikely. Three: she went to the hotel in order to meet a friend or relative."

"She has no close relatives," said the man. "As for friends, why would she not tell me?"

"Four: she went there to meet a publisher. Is she interested in becoming a published writer?"

"Well, yes, as it happens. However, I do not think she will succeed. Her work is too avant-garde."

"Have you told her such?"

"Yes. I may have even spoken disparagingly of her work."

"Then that would explain why she did not tell you of her activities."

"Yes, that is possible."

"So, so far we have two possibilities: that your wife has a lover; that she is an aspiring writer. Let us now consider the other piece of evidence; that she was in possession of a letter that she did not wish you to see. As yet, we do not know if she was the writer of the letter or the recipient."

"Oh, she was definitely the recipient. It was written in a huge, vulgar scrawl. That much I was able to observe. My wife's handwriting is very small – so small that you almost need a magnifying glass to read it."

"Very well. Now; let us list the possibilities as to who this letter might be from."

"I thought we had already listed the possibilities."

"The events of the letter and the visit to the hotel may be entirely unconnected. As far as the letter is concerned, your suggestion that she is involved in an illicit liaison is indeed possible. However, as with the other piece of evidence, there are other possibilities. The letter may have been a rejection from a publisher."

"Not the publisher idea again."

"So you see, Mr. Antonio, both pieces of evidence support the idea that she is attempting to become a published writer. This possibility must be eliminated. If you were to discuss with your wife her writing career, she may enable you to do so."

"I shall return home and check your 'possibility'," said the man. "If it turns out to be impossible, I shall return."

"You are quite welcome to do so," said Holmes.

*

"Occupation? I have no occupation," said the third client of the day, seated in the usual armchair. "I am of independent means. Not that my means are anything more than modest."

He was a poetic man who had the indifferent manner of one who does not have to make his own way in the world. "I moved to the East End of London because it is cheap," he said.

"A colourful area," said Holmes.

"That is one way of putting it. It is unusual for such as me to be moving into the area. Most of the long-term residents are moving out. It is rapidly becoming an immigrant ghetto."

"So I have heard," said Holmes.

"I have rented what might be described as an 'artisan's' house," went on the man. "The previous tenant was evicted. There are two rooms on the upper floor and two on the lower, separated by a narrow, steep staircase. The house lies in a very long row of houses, all identical, with a miniature garden at the back. A wall separates each garden from the next. The houses are each inhabited by what could be as many as twenty people. It can be quite noisy, what with the trains trundling over the railway bridge; however, I have become used to it."

"I take it that something untoward has occurred," said Holmes.

"Yes. Since I moved in, food has begun to disappear from the house. Also candles and even some of my books."

"Could you provide a layout of the house?" enquired Holmes. In my helpful state, I provided the man with pencil and paper.

"There are only two doorways into the house," said

the man, as he drew lines upon the paper. "The front, accessible from the street, which leads directly into the front parlour, and the back, accessible from the garden, which leads directly into the back parlour. There is an alleyway that runs from the street into the back garden, alongside the house underneath the upper floor." He handed Holmes the piece of paper, on which was drawn a rough plan of the lower floor and of the upper, which I here reproduce:

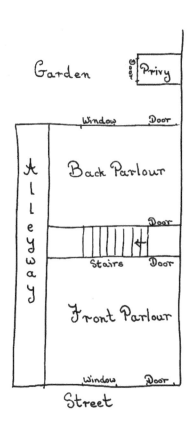

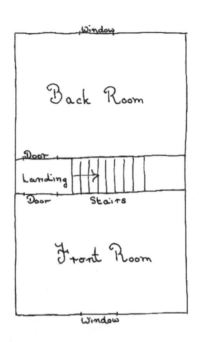

"What about the roof?" asked Holmes. "Is there a skylight?"

"No," said the man. "At least, I do not think so. I have been up in the attic once and could find no skylight or hole in the ceiling. However, it was rather dark up there. I could have missed something."

"Was this during the day?"

"Yes."

"Then presumably there is no skylight or hole, or it would have let the daylight through. How wide is the chimney?"

"No one could get down it, not even a small boy," said the man.

"What about the fireplaces? Could they provide a way into the house?"

"I have come across no such mechanism."

"Trap doors, or doors hidden in the walls?"

"There is no sign of one. The walls and floor are bare."

"Do you at any time leave the doors unlocked?" enquired Holmes.

"Only to use the privy outside at the back of the house."

"Where do you keep your keys?"

"The back door key is always in the lock, inside the house. The front door key I keep on my person or upstairs on a table in the front room."

"And the windows? Are they kept fastened?"

"Whenever I am out of the house, yes."

"Can you describe the circumstances under which some of these thefts have occurred?"

"Yes. It started with carrots and lettuces stolen from my back garden. However, the potatoes were left alone. Then food from inside the house began to disappear. On one occasion, I went out early on an errand. While I was out, it rained heavily. When I returned, I came in through the alleyway to use the privy. I found some muddy footprints upon the path in my garden, leading up to the back door and back again. They were the footprints of a barefoot child. Despite the fact that the back door was locked, I found these same footprints in the parlour. On examining the pantry I found that some bread and meat was missing."

"Were footprints found anywhere else in the house?" asked Holmes.

"No. They were confined to the back parlour."

"And your books? In what manner did they disappear?"

"Again, it was in the morning when I was out. I had

left a book on the table in the front parlour, clearly visible from outside. When I returned, it was gone, as were the candles from the candelabra."

"It would appear that the appropriator was an intellectual," said Holmes.

"A book can be sold," said the man.

"Indeed. Does that complete your report of the thefts?"

"No. After the first few thefts occurred, I was anxious to increase security. I took the step of installing window locks on the downstairs windows. I also ceased to leave the key in the back door. Instead, I took it with me whenever I went out. Thinking that that would be the end of the trouble, you can imagine how put out I was when I returned to the house one afternoon to find a ladder, leaning against the wall at the back of the house. It led up to the upstairs window, which was open. I went upstairs, fearing the worst, but could find no one up there. What is more, nothing was taken, despite the fact that there were objects of value in the rooms. That I do not understand. Nevertheless, I feel quite violated. It would seem that there is no way to avoid these burglaries, other than to move to a better area. However, I have signed a six month contract, and doing so would lose me rather a lot of money."

"There is no need for concern, Mr. Cordell," said Holmes. "The extensiveness of your information provides an obvious solution."

"Well, it is not obvious to me," said Mr. Cordell.

"There is, as far as I can see, only one possible explanation for the events that you have described," went on Holmes. "Your burglar is coming from inside the house, rather than outside."

"Inside the house? There is no one inside the house but me."

"I think you will find that you are sharing the house with another. Consider the facts: footprints were found on the garden path that mysteriously rematerialized in the back parlour, despite the barrier of the locked door. The owner of the footprints had no way to access the key on the inside of the door: there was no gap underneath the door; no glass broken; no way to fit a key into the lock, for there was already a key there. Therefore there is only one possibility: the owner of the footprints was let into the house by another. That other was not you."

"Good Heavens, Mr. Holmes," said the man. "Who was this 'other'? And what about the ladder? Surely that indicates that someone was trying to get into the house from outside."

"It could indicate that. It could also indicate that someone was trying to get out of the house from the inside. After you had put window locks on all the downstairs windows, and removed the key to the back door, there was no way to get out of the house except through the windows on the upper floors."

"But I never had a ladder," objected the man. "Where did it come from?"

"From the attic," said Holmes. "Which is where you will find your illicit lodger."

Mr. Cordell was rendered speechless.

"But even if there were a 'lodger' hiding in my attic, why would they wish to leave the house?" he asked, presently. And how would they get back in?"

"The sight of your lettuces must have been too much of a temptation," said Holmes. "They would be out only for a short time and would get back in the way they came. In fact, you have probably locked the poor individual out of your house. The ladder would not have been there when you returned, had they succeeded in getting back into the house and back in the attic."

"But who was the owner of the footprints leading up to my back door?"

"One of the local children, I expect. Your stowaway must have taken pity on him."

"I shall go straight home and investigate," said the man. "In the company of a police constable. I should never have moved into an immigrant area."

"The stowaway may not have been an immigrant," said Holmes. "We cannot overlook the possibility that it was the previous tenant who has been living in your attic and helping themselves to your food, books and candles. On the day the bailiffs arrived, was the tenant seen to leave?"

"No. According to the next door neighbours, he had already gone when they arrived."

"Did they say where?"

"No. Nobody saw him leaving the area at any time, as far as I know. He may have done a moonlight flit."

"That is not usual if it has come to bailiffs," said Holmes. "In that situation, the tenant usually stays in the property for as long as possible. The fact that he was not there is a peculiarity and strengthens the hypothesis that at the time that the bailiffs arrived, he was hiding somewhere in the house."

"I will let you know if you are right," said the man, standing up. "Here is your fee. Now, I am anxious to return home. A very good day to you, Mr. Holmes." The man exited the room with an energetic step, closing the door behind him.

"Judging from the rate at which you solve other people's mysteries, you can have none of your own," I said, when he had left.

"I am always mystified by coincidence," said Holmes. "It was indeed a coincidence that I should happen to meet you on the very day that you were so needed. I had all but given up hope of taking these rooms, in the absence of one to go halves with. It was an example of serendipity, a strange and yet real phenomenon."

"It was an encouraging day for me too," I said. "For the idea of leaving the metropolis and rusticating somewhere in the country did not appeal."

Holmes stood up from his armchair by the fire and reached for the Persian slipper on the mantelpiece. He recharged his pipe with the strongest tobacco, lit it, and amidst puffs of smoke, went into his own chamber. He did not emerge until two hours later, when Mrs. Hudson entered the sitting-room, carrying a sweeping brush and carpet cleaner.

"Oh, I do apologize, Mr. Holmes," she said. "I had thought you would have gone out by this time."

"I may have more clients during the course of the afternoon," said Holmes. "In the evening, however, we shall most probably be out."

Mrs. Hudson left and closed the door, only to appear again a few moments later, in the company of the Italian gentleman whose acquaintance we had made that morning.

"Your client has returned," she said.

The Italian gentlemen re-entered the room and sat

back down in the clients' chair without invitation.

"You were right, Mr. Holmes," he began, at once. "My wife is an aspiring writer. The letter was a rejection from a publisher, and the visit to the hotel, an appointment with a publisher. She prefers to meet publishers in a public place, rather than in their office. The evidence is explained. However, this does not prove that she has no lover."

"But you now have no evidence for that," said Holmes.

"Even if I have no evidence, it proves nothing," said the man. "Can you prove to me that she does not have a lover?"

"What do you mean by a lover?" asked Holmes. "An annual meeting of a romantic nature? A romance by letter? A fantasy figure? Would any of these be included in your definition of a lover?"

"I mean a person whom she is meeting on a regular basis."

"Only twenty-four hour surveillance of your wife could determine that," said Holmes. "An area in which I do not specialize. There are plenty in London who do."

"I shall not sink as low as that," said the man. "Perhaps I am behaving in an overly jealous fashion. I shall try to forget all about it."

"That I would advise," I said. The Italian glanced at me, with an expression to suggest that he had not asked for my opinion. He then turned back to Holmes.

"Should I require your help, may I count on your further assistance?" he enquired.

"Naturally," said Holmes.

"Then I shall not take up any more of your invaluable time." He stood up to leave and went over to the door. "Perhaps we shall meet again, at one of my wife's concerts," he said, bowing slightly. As he exited he was met by someone on the landing. "Oh, excuse me," he said, and he was gone. Holmes went over to the door whereupon I recognized the familiar voice of the pageboy as he announced a telegram delivery.

Holmes closed the door again. "It is from Mrs. Wellesley," he said, handing me the communication. It displayed just three words:

KEY FOUND. ELLA.

"Perhaps I should keep a record of your cases," I said. "I could even write a report of them and submit them to a magazine."

"By all means, do," said Holmes. "I shall read them with interest."

I did not mention that should I write these reports, they would not read in the style of a scientific paper, for the simple reason that scientific papers do not sell. Explaining that to Holmes might have proven difficult, and was better put off until the need arose.

The Duchess' Diamonds

It was not usual for Holmes to receive visitors at his rooms in Baker Street on a non-professional basis. Still more unusual was it for relatives to call; his brother Mycroft had been at our lodgings on only one occasion. I was therefore more than a little surprised when one afternoon a young gentleman who turned out to be Holmes' first cousin appeared at the door of our sitting-room.

"Raffles!" exclaimed Holmes, and stepped aside to let the gentleman in. "How long has it been? You were in the eleven at school when I last saw you."

The visitor entered the room, smiling. He had the appearance of a carefree man-about-town but there was a certain preoccupied tension in his manner.

"I am residing at the Albany," he said. "I haven't been there long. I don't know too many in the capital and thought I might look you up."

"Well, you are most welcome," said Holmes. "Do sit down."

Raffles sank into an armchair and took from his inner pocket a silver cigarette case engraved with a Tudor rose. He lit up one of the cigarettes contained therein and slid the case over the table to Holmes and me. The

cigarettes were Sullivans; the visitor was indeed a gentleman. Amidst puffs of smoke, I was able to observe him
more closely. There was something unscrupulous about
the cold blue eye and rigid jaw and yet I felt that I would
have trusted him further than many others. He did not
seem like someone who liked to indulge in idle chit-chat;
I wondered why he had come to see Holmes.

"Not a bad pad you have here, Holmes," said Raffles,
glancing briefly around. "You appear to have moved up
in the world."

"Indeed," said Holmes. "My consulting business, as
you might call it, has prospered. I began as an unknown
but I believe I am now the most famous detective in
London, if not the world."

"Which is why I was able to find you so easily," said
Raffles. "I have not done too badly myself, either. There
is not one in the cricket world who has not heard of A.J.
Raffles."

"How do you live out of the cricket season?" enquired
Holmes.

"In the manner of a gentleman," replied Raffles, leaning back in the armchair. "Unlike you, I have not sunk
to the ranks of the middle-classes but have kept up the
social standing from which we both descend."

"I have done quite well enough by my own efforts to
live like a gentleman," said Holmes, stiffly. "I merely
choose not to. My brain would stagnate if subjected to a
useless, idle life. I would be compelled to indulge in what
Watson would call my self-destructive habit. No, the fall
from social standing was to me a godsend. However, I
am puzzled as to how you have succeeded in maintain-
ing yours. The money in our immediate family was not

substantial and most of it went to our eldest cousin. I shall not ask you how you have come to match the lifestyle of our ancestors."

"I knew I could rely on you not to ask," said Raffles. "Just as I know that I can always rely on you." He got up and went over to the window. Concealed by the curtain that hung on one side he stared cautiously out into the street.

"Is anything the matter?" asked Holmes.

Raffles turned to face him. "No, nothing at all," he said. "I've just remembered I have an appointment at twelve. I trust you will not be averse to my calling on you again in the near future."

"No, not at all," said Holmes. "You are always welcome here."

Taking one more look out of the window, Raffles departed as abruptly as he had come. As his footsteps faded away, I turned to my friend in amazement.

"Well," I said. "What an extraordinary character."

"Quite," said Holmes. "Would you believe, I have not seen him for ten years. He was colourful enough then, and more so now, I would say."

"Did you not think that his behaviour was a little strange?" I began. "Edgy and unstable, if you know what I mean."

"It certainly was," said Holmes. "And most probably for a good reason. He did not come here merely to reunite with his relative, of that I am sure."

"Then why?"

"He may have required my assistance."

"But he did not ask for it."

"Exactly. Therefore, either he changed his mind about

asking for it, or he obtained it without asking for it. I suspect the latter."

"In what way could he have obtained your assistance?"

"He may have dumped something here that he did not wish to lose or to be found on his person."

"Dumped something? You mean, loot?"

"Precisely, Watson. As you know, I am well acquainted with Inspector Lestrade of Scotland Yard. Although I have been more use to him than he to me, he has been good enough from time to time to inform me of goings-on in the police force. And I am privy to the information that the CID has the gravest suspicions concerning my cousin the cricketer."

"Suspicions? You mean that your cousin is a criminal?"

"Suspected criminal, yes, Watson. As yet, they have no evidence other than circumstantial evidence. I too, have my suspicions, despite the fact that he is my cousin. I believe that he is as adept as covering his tracks as I would be at uncovering them, were I to take on the case. However, that I would never do for he is my cousin."

At this moment the door to the sitting-room opened. "Inspector Mackenzie to see you," announced Mrs. Hudson.

An inspector whom I had never met before entered the room without ado. He took one look at me and then turned to Holmes.

"You are Mr. Holmes, I take it," he began, in a pronounced Scottish accent.

"Quite so," said Holmes. He stood facing the inspector but did not offer him a seat. An embarrassing silence followed. Finally, the inspector spoke again.

"Has Mr. Raffles been here?" he asked.

"My cousin did pay us a visit today," replied Holmes.

"Did he perchance leave anything with you? Such as a box or case of any kind?"

"He came with nothing and went with nothing."

Inspector Mackenzie appeared dissatisfied. He looked all around the room and then walked over to the corner cupboard. He was about to open it when Holmes stopped him.

"Do you have a warrant, Inspector?"

"No, said Mackenzie, retreating. "However, you cannot object to me taking a look around. An item of considerable value has been stolen from a train carriage in Euston Station."

"I'm afraid I do object," said Holmes. "I am most particular about my possessions. I will not allow even Mrs. Hudson to go sorting through my things. If you really believe that an antique or whatever it is you are looking for is concealed on these premises you will have to go through the proper procedure. In any case, I assure you, there is nothing of any interest in that cupboard." Holmes turned the key that was positioned in the lock and put it in his pocket.

"I always did hold the view that you had a sneaking disregard for the law," said Mackenzie. "If you are covering up for your cousin, you will find yourself in trouble of the most serious kind."

"As you will be, should you deviate from protocol," said Holmes. "I shall be watching you closely, Mackenzie."

Inspector Mackenzie appeared uncertain as to his next move. "If your cousin returns, please inform the Yard immediately," he said, and then departed in a huffy manner. We heard the front door slam after which Mrs. Hudson entered the room directly.

"Should I have let him in, sir?" she asked, tentatively. "He did not have a warrant."

"Yes, you should have," said Holmes. "I have never before refused entry to an officer of the law and do not intend to start now. However, should he return without a warrant whilst we are out, do not permit him to search this room."

"No, sir," said Mrs. Hudson, whereupon she left the room again.

"Do you really think that the 'loot' is hidden somewhere in this room?" I asked, in an inappropriately excited tone. "Your cousin hardly had any chance to conceal it." I went over to the armchair where Raffles had been seated and lifted up the cushion, but nothing was there.

"Nevertheless, I am convinced that it is here," said Holmes. "And we must find it quickly. It is possible that Mackenzie will succeed in obtaining a search warrant, despite having no evidence other than his own paranoid suspicions."

"We don't even know what we are looking for," I said, at which Holmes went over to the fireplace and took the morning's newspaper out from the rack. Glancing over the front page, he directed me to a notice in the stop-press.

JEWEL ROBBERY IN LONDON

Last night between seven and eight p.m. a theft of jewels belonging to the Dowager Duchess of Strathclyde occurred from a first-class compartment in a train at Euston Station bound for Aberdeen.

"As we might expect, it is jewels of some description that we are seeking," he said to me and immediately began to search around the room, however to no avail. I joined in his search but found myself to be equally unsuccessful.

"It would appear that my cousin has hidden the case rather too well," said Holmes. "But as you say, he was in no more than three places during his brief visit here: in the armchair, by the window and outside the door."

"Why did you tell the inspector that your cousin had been here?"

"There was no point in denying it. Raffles was undoubtedly seen entering the premises. Take a look outside the window, Watson."

I went over to where Raffles had stood and looked out into the street. What was presumably one of Mackenzie's men was lounging about in the guise of a loafer on the opposite pavement.

"It would appear that the house is being watched," I observed.

"Quite so, Watson. It is not just Raffles that they are watching. We, too, are under surveillance as possible accessories to the crime."

A vision of a cell in Pentonville prison flashed briefly before me. "It is absolutely imperative that we find those jewels," I said. "For our own sake if not Raffles'." I went outside onto the landing and searched in the coat pockets that hung by the door. The umbrella stand was empty save for Holmes' cane and my umbrella. The cane was a loadable one but the barrel was empty. My own umbrella concealed nothing. A thorough examination of the potted plant that stood beside the door proved equally fruitless. I was about to go back into the sitting-room when a thought struck me; I called down the stairs for Mrs. Hudson, who came up once again. When she arrived, she seemed a little fed up with having to walk up and down the stairs ten times a day.

"Mrs. Hudson," I asked, without delay. "Did Mr. Raffles at any time have the opportunity to enter any of the rooms in your private areas?"

"No, he did not," replied Mrs. Hudson. "He just came straight up here."

"And on leaving?"

"He just came straight down again and out of the door."

"Oh," I said, despondently. The problem now seemed to be logically impossible. "I don't suppose he gave you a case or item of any kind?"

"Certainly not," said Mrs. Hudson. "I would have informed you."

"Yes, I suppose you would," I said.

"Will there be anything else?" asked Mrs. Hudson

"No, I should think we can manage for the rest of the day without your help," said Holmes, at which Mrs. Hudson left the room for the third time that morning.

I continued my assiduous search but on finding nothing during the course of the next hour, began to wonder if Raffles' visit had not been merely of the social kind. Holmes appeared to have given up and was now engaged in his laboratory work. In the early afternoon the heavy tread of Mackenzie's footsteps was heard once more advancing up the stairs to the first floor landing. It was accompanied by other footsteps of an equally hefty nature. Finally, Mackenzie entered the room, three uniformed officers behind him.

"You are usually very lucky, Mr. Holmes, very lucky," he said, as Holmes looked up from his laboratory. "I will give you that. But today, I am afraid, you are out of luck." He held up a folded piece of white paper. "You see, the judge presiding at the court today has a wife who is a friend of the wife of one of the inspectors at the yard. He was quite easily persuaded to give out a warrant. I therefore have the authority to search this room." He nodded to the three constables, who, armed with implements of various kinds, began a very thorough search of the room. Mackenzie himself did not participate, but stood expectantly in observation.

"I shall hold you personally responsible for any damage done in the process," said Holmes, as the constables began to open up the cushions in the armchairs and lifting the rugs that covered the floorboards. "I hope you realize that there are valuable items of furniture in this room."

"Not as valuable as the item that I am looking for," said Mackenzie.

"What makes you think that you will find it here?" asked Holmes.

"Mr. Raffles your cousin was seen entering these premises. We caught up with him shortly after he left here, but found nothing on him. It therefore seems highly probable that he deposited the item that we are looking for here."

"Assuming that he was in possession of it in the first place."

"Which I am," said Mackenzie.

I watched as the search continued. Apart from tearing up the plaster, nothing was left untouched. The detective-inspector continued to display a confident attitude; however as time dragged on he became pensive.

"There's nothing here," said one of the men, finally.

Mackenzie appeared puzzled and annoyed. However, without any fuss or bother, he departed from our rooms for the second time that day. We watched from the window as he and the loafer across the street went on their way. I half expected Mackenzie to return in the next five minutes in an attempt to catch Holmes red-handed with the loot, but such an event never occurred. For the remainder of the hour I could not help to look out of the window repeatedly, but nothing untoward came to pass. That was, until after six o'clock, when the distinct figure of Raffles suddenly appeared walking up the street and crossing over near to our lodgings.

"Your cousin is back," I said, turning to Holmes, who sat reading the evening newspaper by the fire like a middle-class office clerk.

Holmes looked around. "It is as would be expected," he said.

"He must have come to collect the loot," I said. "Though I cannot imagine where it might be."

Raffles appeared in the room again, this time in immaculate evening dress. He gazed around at the disarray left by Mackenzie and his men.

"I take it you had a visit from some official people," he said.

"We did. Take a seat."

Raffles sat down in the same armchair as before. "You left your cigarette case behind," said Holmes, handing the article to his cousin.

"So I did," said Raffles, immediately putting it away

in his pocket. "I hope I haven't inconvenienced you in any way."

"Not at all," said Holmes. "However, it might be better if any future meetings were to take place outside of these rooms."

"Of course," said Raffles. "I expect to be in London over the summer. However, the places in which I move may be a little too grand for you. I am not often seen in a coffee-house unless it is located in the city."

"Oh, that does not worry me at all," said Holmes. "I am quite used to associating with the grandest of society."

II

"I note that Inspector Mackenzie has not been round here to apologize," I said at breakfast a few days later.

"And he will not," said Holmes. "I believe he is the only inspector at Scotland Yard who would not shake my hand."

It was then a case of 'speak of the devil and the devil will appear', for within half-a-minute of my mentioning his name, the man himself appeared in our sitting-room. However, instead of the threatening stance that he had previously taken, his manner was now polite and cordial.

"Mr. Holmes," said Mackenzie in a friendly tone. "I do apologize for last week's fiasco. As the theft of the jewels had all the hall-marks of your cousin's work, I jumped to the conclusion that he was responsible. As it turns out he was at a country weekend party in Reigate at the time, so could not have been involved in any way."

"I take it that the jewels are still at large," said Holmes.

"You are right, Mr. Holmes," said Mackenzie. "I have made absolutely no progress in the case whatsoever. I was wondering ..."

"If I might be able to shed some light?"

"Yes. I have heard from Gregson and Lestrade of your extraordinary capacity to fathom the unfathomable although I never really believed it myself. However, as we at the Yard appear to have reached an impasse as far as this case is concerned I thought that there might be no harm in asking your opinion on it."

"What is the estimated value of the jewels?" asked Holmes.

"Between twenty and twenty-five thousand pounds," said Mackenzie.

"And the type of jewel?"

"A diamond necklace consisting of stones of varying sizes."

"Are the diamonds identifiable?"

"There are photographs of them taken at close range," said Mackenzie.

"Good. Then an attempt at their recovery will not be a complete waste of time. Has a reward been offered?"

"No. The Duchess refuses point blank to give a penny to the criminal class. However, I might add, should you succeed in recovering the diamonds, she might not prove ungenerous."

"I shall bear that in mind," said Holmes. "Are the exact circumstances in which the diamonds were stolen known to you?"

"Yes," said Mackenzie. "The Duchess had arranged to meet her husband at Euston station on Saturday evening last. On her arrival at the station she instructed her maid to place the jewel-case in the compartment in which she would be travelling. The Duchess remained on the platform close to the carriage door and did not move from that position except to meet her husband, and even then no more than a couple of yards. It is therefore assumed that the thieves came in either through the door at the other end of the carriage or down the corridor."

"Was anything else stolen at the time?"

"Yes. The Duchess' satchel, containing two notes of value five pounds and ten pounds."

"Is the maid implicated in any way?"

"No," replied Mackenzie. "Neither is the valet who was accompanying the party."

"Was the robbery planned, in your opinion?"

"No. We believe the theft to have been of a spontaneous and opportunistic nature."

Holmes considered this. "At what point was the theft noticed?"

"The Duchess' party was already on its way to Aberdeen by the time it was noticed."

"So it is possible that the diamonds were stolen after the train left."

"No. The Duchess was in the compartment from the moment the train left until the theft was discovered."

"Is it certain that the diamonds were actually stolen? Have you eliminated the possibility of insurance fraud?"

"The diamonds were not insured. The Duchess never insures anything that she can afford to replace, which is most things."

"And you are quite sure that my cousin is no longer a suspect in this case."

"Oh, yes," said Mackenzie. "He was seen to be present

at the house of Sir Robert Reynolds between seven-thirty and nine-thirty on Saturday evening. There are scores of witnesses to substantiate this fact. However, it is now believed that he may have committed some indiscretion at that particular place; an antique silver cigarette case engraved with a Tudor rose was found to be missing on the Monday morning after he left."

"I do not feel able to help you in the recovery of the cigarette case," said Holmes. "However, I would be happy to devote my attention to the diamonds. Would it be possible for me to interview the Duchess?"

"The Duchess is in Inverness-shire," said Mackenzie. "However, it should be possible to arrange for you to speak to her on the telephone."

"I think that may be the best solution," said Holmes.

"Very well. I shall contact you by telegram to inform you when the Duchess will be available. Are there any other lines of investigation that you wish to pursue?"

"The Duchess' hotel room," said Holmes. "Would it be possible for me to examine it?"

"Under the orders of Scotland Yard, I would think so," said Mackenzie. "Though what you hope to achieve by that, I cannot imagine. The diamonds were stolen between seven and eight o'clock in the evening at Euston Station. I would consider the Duchess' hotel room to be completely irrelevant."

"Nevertheless," said Holmes.

"Very well," said Mackenzie. "I shall make the necessary arrangements for that, too." He made a brief note in his pocket book. "Anything else?"

"No, I believe that is all for the moment," said Holmes.

*

Mackenzie's office was situated in one of the turrets of the gothic building on the Victoria embankment that houses the headquarters of the Metropolitan police. Overlooking the river, it was lavishly furnished with a carpet and a large mahogany desk on which was positioned a newly installed telephone. We sat opposite the detective inspector as he conversed with the operator.

"If you will just wait a moment, it will take a little while for the operators to patch up," said Mackenzie, replacing the receiver. "Would you like a cup of coffee, Mr. Holmes?"

"No, thank you," said Holmes.

"Or you, Mr. Watson?"

I also declined. The luxurious ambience of the workplace seemed to suit Mackenzie; his manner was debonair, as though he believed he had found his true place at last. It was however without a doubt that his elevation to the higher echelons of the police force had been, as in the case of Gregson and Lestrade, a laborious procedure. It was becoming difficult to think of something to say. I could have asked him about the photographs on his desk but did not, for fear of saying the wrong thing. At last, the telephone rang. Mackenzie immediately picked up the receiver. After a moment he handed it to Holmes.

"The Duchess is on the line. Go ahead, Mr. Holmes."

Holmes took the receiver from Mackenzie and spoke on the telephone for what may have been the very first time. "This is Mr. Sherlock Holmes," he said, clearly and a little louder than usual. "Am I addressing the Duchess?"

"You are," came a distant voice that I too could hear.

"I have been asked by Inspector Mackenzie of Scotland Yard to look into the theft of your diamond necklace.

Would it be inappropriate for me to ask Your Grace a couple of questions?"

"No, it would be most appropriate."

"Could you tell me exactly when you last saw the diamonds – the actual necklace itself, not just the case."

"It was at about a quarter past six - just before we were due to leave for the station," said the Duchess. "I instructed my maid to place them in the jewel case, which she duly did. I observed her do it. We then travelled down to the station in a taxi, taking the case and my satchel with us."

"How long did you stay at the hotel?"

"One week."

"Where did you keep the diamonds during your stay?"

"I collected them from the bank on the Saturday morning before we were due to leave. In the afternoon, they were in the hotel suite."

"Did you at any time leave them unattended in the hotel suite?"

"No. I was there all afternoon, writing letters."

"Did anyone enter the room while you were there?"

"No, apart from my maid. I had sent her out to run some errands for me."

"Are you sure?"

"Quite sure. I would know if anyone else had entered because the door to the suite led into the sitting-room, where I was."

"Hello? Hello?" Holmes replaced the receiver. "It would appear we have been disconnected," said Holmes.

"Would you like me to arrange a re-connection?" asked Mackenzie.

"No, I have already heard all I need to know. If I could visit the Duchess' hotel room."

"Certainly," said Mackenzie. "We can go now, if you like."

"That would be most efficient," said Holmes. We followed Mackenzie out into the broad corridor and down a stone flight of stairs leading to a little back door, through which we left the building. Once out in the street again we hailed a four wheeler. It took us directly north, cutting through the centre of London and into Bloomsbury.

The Langham hotel is a fine building, facing up Portland Place towards Regent's Park. It is notable not just for its grandiosity but for its clientele, which has included Oscar Wilde and Toscanini as well as members of the Royal Houses of Europe. Those who wish for a glimpse of the rich and famous can achieve this aim by taking tea in the lounge, or even just standing by when the objects of admiration step out of their opulent coaches and enter the hotel through its flagged portico. On arrival at this location we were permitted to go through into the luxuriant foyer, where we were greeted by a footman who at once showed us up to the apartment in question. The suite consisted of a sitting-room and bedchamber similar to our own in Baker Street. It was not currently occupied.

"Very refined, I must say," I said, viewing the elegant, Chippendale furniture and flowered wallpaper.

"It is our best suite," said the footman. "Reserved for only the most exalted of guests."

"Evidently," said Holmes. "Is this the writing desk at which the Duchess wrote her letters?"

"Your guess is as good as mine, sir," said the footman.

"It faces the door of the suite," said Holmes. "Presumably the Duchess would have noticed if someone had walked in. May I take a look in the bedchamber?"

"By all means," said the footman, leading the way into the second room, in which a four poster bed of Elizabethan design took pride of place. Holmes glanced briefly around. He opened the drawers of the dresser and wardrobe but other than that, showed little interest.

"There is nothing more for me to do here," said Holmes, surprisingly. Mackenzie reacted in an indifferent manner. "We had better go back down again, then," he concluded. The four of us traipsed out of the suite and into the lift again, where we were taken back down to the expansive and elegant entrance hall.

"Well, Mr. Holmes," began Mackenzie, as we stood outside the grand hotel once more. "Have you come to any conclusions?

"You were right," said Holmes. "The hotel suite is completely irrelevant. I only asked to see it because it was the one stone left unturned."

"Quite so, Mr. Holmes," said Inspector Mackenzie. "I admire your attention to detail. What do you propose to do now?"

"I am very much afraid that the thieves have got clean away. You might be well-advised not to waste too much time on this case."

"You may have given up," said Mackenzie. "However, I have no intention of doing so. I am a tenacious and persistent man, Mr. Holmes."

"I can well believe it. Well, if you have no further business with me, let us part company. I am sure you have much to attend to, Mackenzie," said Holmes.

"I do," said Mackenzie. "Good-day, Mr. Holmes, and thank you for your time." He raised his hat and then walked off into the hubbub of London.

"It's not like you to give up so easily," I said, when he had gone.

"No," said Holmes. "Let us go back into the hotel. I have one matter to attend to."

I followed my friend into the entrance hall again and up to the reception.

"Inspector Mackenzie has instructed that I may conduct my own investigation here," said Holmes. "I would like to see the guest book."

The attendant took a large ledger book from behind the counter and placed it before Holmes, who at once began turning the pages. He stopped at one near the end of the entries, then closed the book again. "Thank you very much," he said and walked out of the hotel again.

"Well?" I enquired.

"There was a Mr. Alistair residing in the room adjacent to the Duchess on the afternoon in question," he said.

"I am afraid I am as baffled as Mackenzie as to why you are so interested in hotel rooms," I said. "The diamonds were last seen just before the Duchess and her maid left for the station."

"Indeed they were," said Holmes. "However, I am haunted by Mackenzie's remark that the theft has all the hallmarks of my cousin's work. That, I feel, carries more weight than the Duchess' testimony. I am now going on the premise that Raffles was indeed responsible. He is known to have been in Reigate at the time that the theft is supposed to have occurred, therefore I deduce from the premise that the theft did not occur then."

"But you cannot go on such a premise," I said. "If the diamonds were in the case at a quarter past six then Raffles could not have taken them."

"There may be an explanation for that," said Holmes. "I will come to it later."

"All right," I said, finally. "Let us suppose that Raffles did take the diamonds. How exactly did he go about it?"

"He came into the bedroom of the Duchess' hotel suite at some point during the afternoon."

"And how, pray, did he do that? The Duchess was there the whole time and was quite sure that no one came into the hotel suite."

"He did not enter the suite through the main door. He came in through the interconnecting door linking the Duchess' bedroom to the adjacent suite."

"What interconnecting door?"

"The one that was clearly apparent when we were up in the bedroom just now."

"I did not notice it."

"Neither did Mackenzie, I am glad to say," said Holmes.

"I will take your word for it that it was there," I said. "However, I thought you said that the room adjacent to the Duchess was occupied by a Mr. Alistair."

"It was, Watson."

"Then how could Raffles have been occupying it?"

"I am very much afraid that Raffles and Mr. Alistair are one and the same," said Holmes. "The address given in the hotel guest book had the London postcode of N.E., which does not exist. As for the signature, the flourishing 'A' of Alistair was almost identical to that of my cousin's portrayal of his initial, 'A'. What is more, Mr. Alistair checked out that very afternoon."

"I doubt if Mackenzie will discover that," I said.

"I would not be too sure," said Holmes. "Mackenzie

is not completely incompetent. I would put him above Gregson and Lestrade. It may not be too long before the wheels turn over and he realizes that Raffles could have been involved in the theft of the Duchess' diamonds after all."

Much as I doubted Mackenzie's expertise, it was not more than a few days before I was to see the detective inspector again. I had gone out to purchase some stationery and was a little disturbed to find Mackenzie there when I got back.

"Oh, hello, Mr. Mackenzie," I said, unenthusiastically. "How is the case going?"

"There has been a development," said Mackenzie. "Both the jewel case and the satchel belonging to the Duchess have turned up at the lost property office at Euston. They were handed in by a passenger who found them discarded at the other end of the station. As you might expect, the money in the satchel was gone. The diamonds, however, were still in the case. The only problem is, they were paste."

"Paste?" I repeated.

"Indeed," said Mackenzie. "I have been asking your friend's thoughts on the matter. However, he appears not to have any. What do you think, Mr. Watson?"

"The Duchess had not realized that her diamonds were paste," I said.

"That is the view that Scotland Yard is inclined to take," said Mackenzie. "They had not been assessed by a professional jeweller for many years. However, on the way home last night it suddenly occurred to me that the diamonds could have been switched for paste at some point during the Saturday afternoon."

"That is very fanciful," I said.

"Maybe," said Mackenzie. "However, unlike the other inspectors at Scotland Yard, I have taken note of Mr. Holmes' methods and am now attempting to solve the case using observation and deductive reasoning."

"You are overthinking the problem," said Holmes. "Do you not have a more pressing matter to attend to? Such as a murder or act of treason."

"I shall delegate such tasks to my inferiors," said Mackenzie. "Right now, I am stuck on this."

"Why are you stuck on it?" I asked.

"Because, Mr. Watson, if the real diamonds were taken in the afternoon then your friend Mr. Raffles no longer has his alibi." A satisfied smile came over Mackenzie's features.

"A lack of alibi does not prove guilt," said Holmes.

"I am aware of that," said Mackenzie. "There is more. On realizing that Mr. Raffles was still a possible suspect, I returned to the Langham hotel to gather more evidence. According to the hotel staff, the occupant of the suite adjacent to that of the Duchess had an appearance similar to that of Raffles."

"That of a gentleman, in other words."

"On learning this, I consulted the hotel register. The occupant of that suite was a man who signed himself in as Mr. Alistair, of an address that does not appear to exist. I consulted a handwriting expert who informed me that there were certain similarities between the signature of Mr. Alistair and that of A.J. Raffles."

"That might imply that Mr. Alistair was a gentleman with a similar schooling to Raffles," said Holmes.

"In addition to this," went on Mackenzie. "I found there to be a door interconnecting the Duchess' suite with the adjacent one. The lock on that door was of a primitive design, thereby providing a possible entry route for a possible thief."

"Highly tenuous," said Holmes.

"Maybe," said the detective inspector. "However, I feel confident that I may soon have enough to issue a warrant for his arrest. If he is found guilty, I cannot see him coming out of prison for a very long time. I would estimate seven years hard labour at the very least. A daunting prospect, even for a professional cricketer."

"It is what you have always dreamed of, Mackenzie."

"It is my job to have such dreams," said Mackenzie. "What is more, I no longer require your assistance to realize them. I have overtaken you."

"Have you really."

"Indeed I have, Mr. Holmes. And shall continue to pull ahead. Prepare for greatness." With this, the inspector took his immediate leave.

Holmes went over to the fireplace and loaded his pipe with the strongest tobacco. He lit it and leant musingly against the mantelpiece.

"I am puzzled by the paste," I reflected out loud. "Why would a thief exchange real diamonds for a fake version?"

"In order to prolong the time until the theft was discovered," said Holmes. "But unfortunately for the thief, the paste version was stolen quite by chance a few hours later."

"But how could such a version be created? The thief would have to have exact knowledge of the appearance of the diamonds."

"As could be obtained from the photographs mentioned by Inspector Mackenzie," said Holmes.

"Do you actually buy into this switch theory?"

"The alternative theory is that the Duchess' diamonds were paste all along. That is also possible."

"Without her knowledge? The station thief spotted it pretty quickly."

"It was his habit to spot such things. However, I am inclined to go with the switch theory." Holmes emptied the dregs of his pipe into the fire. "Come, Watson," he said. "Let us not spend Sunday moping in our rooms. There is but a light haze in the atmosphere today – we should be able to see every inch of the Home Counties from the top of the Monument."

Mackenzie was as good as his word. Although too busy in his haute detection to grace us with another visit in person, he materialized again the following week in the form of a telegram, carried by Billy. Holmes took in the contents with a glance and passed it over to me dismissively. It read:

'Fingerprint found in Langham Hotel. Net is closing. Mackenzie.'

"Fingerprints," I exclaimed, putting down my tea. "That could be conclusive."

"It does not say that the fingerprints belong to Raffles," said Holmes. "In any case, fingerprints are not as yet acceptable as evidence in an English court of law."

"Why is he informing you of developments?"

"He wishes to impress upon me how well he is doing," said Holmes. "And to prove his superiority."

"Does this not bode ill for Raffles?"

"My cousin has not been arrested," responded Holmes. "However, I fear that he will be if the diamonds are not recovered very soon."

"That could be difficult," I said. "Presumably they are currently working their way through a trusted route of fences. They are out of your reach."

"Not quite. I will endeavour to get them back."

"And just how do you propose to do that?"

"I will contact Durlston."

"Who is Durlston?"

"Durlston, formerly known to me as Porlock, is a link in those routes of fences to which you refer. If you remember, Watson, Porlock was the weak point of Moriarty's network. Led on by some vague inclination towards right and encouraged by the convenience of an occasional ten-pound note sent to him by devious means he would provide me with information on the Professor's activities from time to time. He was one of the few to escape trial when the entire gang was rounded up, and now works in the pawnbroking business. His strategic position may enable him to purchase the diamonds at the black market price from whomever currently possesses them and resell them to me."

"Won't that cost you, rather?"

"On the contrary, Watson. Diamonds are worth re-markably little on the black market. Many never reach the white market as a jeweller's reputation would be severely damaged were he to be discovered with stolen goods in his stock. I do not expect to have to pay him more than eighty pounds."

"The Duchess will recompense you."

"Maybe. Though it hardly seems appropriate as I have knowledge of the perpetrator."

Holmes was not at the breakfast table on the morning that I received my free monthly copy of the Strand magazine, in which are published my chronicles of Holmes' adventures. He had risen before me and then retreated back into his room. Later on, however, I found him sitting at the table with an opened letter in front of him.

"It is from Durlston," said Holmes. "However, you will not be able to read it. It is written in code."

"Do you have the key to the code?"

"I do. The words in this message all appear in a book that he sent me in the first post. The letter gives the page number, line number and word number in the book for each word in the message. Such a code is primitive, but it has the advantage of being undecipherable without the book."

"Have you deciphered it?"

"I have, Watson. Durlston has the diamonds in his possession and has agreed to sell them to me. He will be here at eleven o'clock this morning."

"I thought that Durlston, formerly Porlock, had defied you to trace him," I said.

"That was in the old days, Watson. I now even know him by his real name. It is true, however, that I have never met him in person. I do not know what he looks like or if he will even come himself, or send another."

"Which side of the law is he on?"

"Neither," said Holmes. "His status lies somewhere in the twilight between right and wrong, as it did when he was a servant of Moriarty."

I began to feel rather curious about our forthcoming

visitor. On the grounds that it was better safe than sorry, I reached for my revolver and placed it in an outer pocket. Holmes, however, seemed less concerned.

At one minute to eleven, the doorbell rang out shrilly. Mrs. Hudson was in to answer it and we listened as a light tread ascended the stairs, unaccompanied by our landlady. Finally there came a quiet knock upon the door.

"Enter," called out Holmes, somewhat unnaturally.

The door opened. Before us stood a figure whose face was disguised by a veil, but was nevertheless identifiable as a woman. She had the appearance of one still young, but something about her suggested her true age. After a furtive look around, she stepped into the room, closing the door behind her.

"You are Porlock!" I exclaimed.

"I am," came a voice from behind the veil. The accent was a neutral one, such as was spoken by myself or Holmes.

"Everything is clear to me now," said Holmes. "To think that all these years, it never once occurred to me that you might not be a man."

"I cannot believe that you were ever in Moriarty's gang," I said.

"Nor was I really," said she. "I was his mistress."

"I suspected that as soon as you walked into this room," said Holmes.

"I didn't know Moriarty had a mistress," I said.

"I was the only one," said she. "Which made it all the more flattering. I could put up with his amoral financial enterprises; but when murder was involved and I was in the knowledge of it, I could not just stand by and do nothing. That is why I would occasionally inform you of whoever was in danger at the time."

"And I always acted accordingly," said Holmes.

"As for the diamonds," went on the woman. "I have them in my possession and can sell them to you for sixty pounds."

"That sounds reasonable," said Holmes. "May I see them?"

"I do not have them on my person," said Porlock. "I presume you wish to return them to the Duchess."

"I do."

"It shall be done," said Porlock. "Upon receipt of the said amount."

Holmes reached over and unlocked the top drawer of the writing desk, from which he took an old-fashioned money box. From this he produced several bank notes and handed them to Porlock. She instantly examined them with a kind of monocle magnifier then put them away in a concealed place somewhere within the copious material of her dress. Then she was gone.

"How could you give her that money?" I asked. "You do not even know that she has the diamonds."

"What would you suggest, Watson? That I hire a solicitor to complete the transaction? She will do as she has said. If not, there will be no future payments."

I wondered if all matters had been concluded. No longer with a case to hand, Holmes began a study of the Brythonic effect on Goidelic languages, considering the merits of the P-Celtic hypothesis over the Insular Celtic hypothesis. Taking advantage of these quiet times, I set about recording some of his more scintillating adventures for future publication. It was some days later that I was in the process of deciding to which case I should next devote my attention when Mrs. Hudson ushered Inspector Mackenzie into our quarters yet again. Holmes was engrossed in the workings of the Celtic Tree Alphabet when he arrived; however, on becoming aware of the inspector's presence, he stopped and greeted him.

"Good afternoon, Mackenzie. What have we done now?"

"Nothing, Mr. Holmes, nothing. I have merely come to inform you that the Duchess' diamonds have been mysteriously returned by an anonymous sender. Much to my dismay, the case is now closed. I advised the Duchess that it should remain open, so that another victim should not fall victim to villainy, but she would not have it. However, I just can't get this diamond business out of my head. I am all but certain that your cousin was involved."

"You must move on, Mackenzie," said Holmes. "By thinking about it you are effectively wasting police time."

"I know, Mr. Holmes," said Mackenzie. "Your cousin will undoubtedly commit further crimes for me to solve. It's just that I was never closer to catching him than I was on this occasion. He was careless, Mr. Holmes. I fear that such an opportunity will not happen again."

"What would you do if you did catch him, Mackenzie?" asked Holmes. "Retire?"

"You are right, Mr. Holmes," said Mackenzie. "There would be nothing left for me. No other crimes have the glamour and ring to them as those of Raffles. I believe him to be world class."

"The fact that you have not caught him does not make him world class," said Holmes.

"You do neither him nor me credit," said Mackenzie.

"He is, however, a world-class cricketer," said Holmes.

"As if you would know," said Mackenzie. "As it happens, I am off to watch him perform this very afternoon."

"Really? Why would you be doing that?"

"I have reason to believe that another robbery is in the offing. No doubt cricket will be his alibi. The Yard may have lost interest in the blackguard but I do not intend to allow him a minute's privacy from now on. The next time he appropriates an article of value I shall be there."

"But what about your work, Mackenzie?"

"I am officially on holiday. For the next two weeks, I am free to do as I please, without instructions from the Chief Inspector."

"What you need is a holiday from Raffles," said Holmes.

The Broken Cartonnage Case

In the last year of the century, early one evening, Holmes received a telegram from the Keeper of Oriental Antiquities at the British Museum, to say that he would be calling on him within the hour.

"You will of course stay and take notes," said Holmes, in a new state of vigour. "There may be much data to record in this case."

This, I felt, would be one of Holmes' more promising cases. A string of illustrious clients had recently come to him for consultation, for his fame was becoming ever wider. However, their cases were not always as illustrious as they were. Holmes was already referring through his expansive filing system, to find whatever he could about our client before he arrived. This index was an oddity in the way Holmes ran his affairs, for they were usually of a disorganized nature.

"Ernest Alfred Thompson Wallis Budge," he read out loud. "An unusually long name for a man of humble origins. Born 1857. Began work as a clerk for W.H.Smith. Learnt Hebrew and Syriac in his spare time. His tutor in these subjects introduced him to the Keeper of Oriental Antiquities at the British Museum, and in 1894, Budge took on that very position himself. Knowledgeable in the Ancient Egyptian language. Well, he appears to have clawed his way up to the higher echelons of society."

"What can he want of you, Holmes?" I asked.

"I never speculate," said Holmes. "When Mr. Budge has laid the facts before me I shall draw my conclusions."

"Egyptology is all the rage at the moment," I said. "Why, only last week there was a report in the newspaper about a 'Mummy's Curse' that has struck down some of the Egyptologists who entered a recently excavated tomb. No less than twenty unexplained deaths have occurred since the tomb was opened."

"No doubt you did not read this in The Times," said Holmes.

"No. It was the D—," I said.

Holmes smiled slightly. "The article concluded with the revelation that curses written in the tombs of the Ancient Egyptians are extremely rare," I added.

"It appears that you have already begun to research into modern Egyptology," said Holmes. "That is good. I may require you to investigate the subject more thoroughly."

"That might suit me," I said. "I sometimes wonder if medicine was the right subject for me. A career in Egyptology could have been the very thing. Why, I excelled in Latin at school. And if this Budge man can rise from the occupation of clerk to a prominent position at the British Museum, I have no excuse. Perhaps I could have obtained a lectureship at one of the smaller universities."

At this moment the sound of a brougham drawing up outside the house interrupted my new train of thought. We waited as Mrs. Hudson let in our client and showed him upstairs. She did not knock but came straight in with him.

Budge was a solidly built man in his forties, dressed in a suit and bow-tie. He viewed Holmes uneasily through his spectacles and looked around the room.

"Do sit down," said Holmes, drawing up an armchair by the fireplace, whereupon he sat down himself. I duly sat down at the writing chair close by and took out my notebook. Budge glanced at me.

"This is my friend and colleague Doctor Watson," said Holmes, as he always did at the beginning of a consultation whenever I was present. "A professional man in his own right, he acts as an invaluable assistant in some of my cases. You may speak in front of him as freely as if we were alone."

I smiled meekly.

"Very well," said Budge. "I take it that everything I say will be kept in the strictest confidence. Of that I have been assured by those who have experience of your work."

"It will," said Holmes.

"A short while ago I returned to London after a visit to Egypt," began Budge. "I had been commissioned by the British Museum to procure artefacts suitable for their collection of Egyptian antiquities. This, my most recent visit, proved to be exceptionally successful. I acquired two sarcophagi of prominent priests, dating from about 800 B.C., as well as numerous amulets and vases. The two sarcophagi arrived at the British Museum a few weeks ago. Each contained a colourfully painted cartonnage case, which in turn, contained a mummy. The sarcophagi had been opened, but the cartonnage cases remained sealed.

They were placed in a chamber in the off-limit areas of the buildings, accessible to only a very few members of staff. The artefacts were locked away in safes, the two sarcophagi laid upon a long table. A guard was posted outside the room at night. Yet on Thursday morning last I received an urgent message from the museum director, informing me that one of the cartonnage cases was now unsealed and the mummy gone." Budge paused.

"But you cannot be held responsible, surely," said Holmes. "There is no cause for alarm on your part."

"Oh, no," said Budge. "However, whenever something of this nature occurs it is always me who has to put it right. I have been instructed by my superiors to recover the mummy. This is not the first time that something like this has happened. A decade ago, I was engaged by the directors of the museum to find out why cuneiforms that were supposedly being guarded by our own agents in Iraq were turning up in the collections of London antiquities dealers. This task occupied me for five whole years. I do not consider it to be the work of a professional Egyptologist. Now it is all happening again. I wish to get to the bottom of this matter as quickly as possible. That is why I have come to you."

"Are these the entire facts?" asked Holmes. "Or is there more to tell me?"

Budge shifted uneasily. "Well, yes there is, but I doubt if you will consider it relevant or even worth listening to."

"That is exactly the sort of fact that interests me," said Holmes. "Pray continue."

"Well, when I arrived at the museum, I went straight

to the director's office. Inside were a couple of other members of staff, and a night guard. He was in quite a shaken and nervous state. After the director had explained to me what had happened, I asked the guard if he had been outside the door of the chamber all night. He said yes, but he must have dozed off for a minute or two, for at around three o'clock in the morning he found the door to the chamber to be slightly ajar. His chair was positioned in a long corridor outside the room and he claims he saw a man bandaged from head to foot walking away at the far end of the corridor. This so terrified him that he could not move from the spot that he was in until dawn and the first member of staff arrived."

I tried not to laugh. "So it is real then," I said.

"What is?" enquired Budge.

"The Curse of the Mummy," I said. "As reported by the D—."

Budge appeared unimpressed. "That rag has been harassing the excavators of our tombs for the last year," he said. "At least the curse story keeps some of our rivals away."

"You do not believe in it yourself?" asked Holmes.

"Of course not. However, I do believe that toxic material may lurk within three thousand year old tombs. That is why I never enter them myself."

"You never enter them yourself?" I gasped. "But you are an Egyptologist."

"Purely on paper," said Budge. "I have written many books on the subject, based on the findings of archaeologists."

"How then, did you acquire the two sarcophagi that you brought back to England?"

"I bought them from a dealer in Cairo. I buy most of the artefacts from local dealers in the neighbouring towns."

"At a reduced rate, I suppose."

"Yes. I have forged ties with the dealers all around that area. That was one of my missions on being sent by the museum to Egypt."

"I see you are quite frank with me," said Holmes. "In turn I shall do my best to put this matter straight. Could you tell me, had any attempt been made to remove the artefacts that were in the safes in the room with the sarcophagi?"

"Yes," said Budge. "But they were unsuccessful."

"So if the mummy were physically removed by another party, their interest was not confined to the mummy."

"What about the guard's story?" I said. "According to his testament, the mummy broke out of its cartonnage case and walked out of the room."

"He was probably dreaming," said Budge. "Or hallucinating. I should not have told you that part of the story."

"Would it be possible for me to pay a visit to the off-limit areas of the museum to perform an examination?" asked Holmes.

"Yes, of course. I have it in my power to authorize that."

"Good. Then if it is convenient we could go along there now; or if not, early tomorrow morning. I might like to interview the guard as well if that is possible."

"I should think that that could be arranged," said the Keeper of Oriental Antiquities. "The guard should be on duty this evening, from around six o'clock."

"Then let us not delay," said Holmes. "Watson and I shall take a hansom to the museum."

"Don't be silly," said Budge. "My carriage is waiting."

The brougham in which we travelled was quite plush inside. It appeared that Budge had done well out of his books and procurement of antiquities.

"Have there been any other thefts of a similar nature to this one that you know of?" asked Holmes, as we sat opposite Budge, who faced the direction of travel.

"Now that you mention it, yes," said Budge. "The mummy of Neskhonspakhered has also vanished. It disappeared at some point whilst it was in transit from Egypt to America. It was not noticed until its arrival at a museum in California that the cartonnage case within the sarcophagus was no longer sealed up."

"Neskhonspakhered," reiterated Holmes.

"The wife of Nesperennub, a priest in Ancient Egypt. The two sarcophagi that I brought back from Egypt were that of Nesperennub and his father, Ankhefenkhons. It is the mummy of Ankhefenkhons that has gone missing."

"So the two disappearances could be connected."

"Yes," said Budge.

"What is your own theory on this matter?" asked Holmes.

"My theory is that the mummy was stolen to order for a private collector."

"Why did they not take the sarcophagus and cartonnage case?"

"They would be very easily identifiable."

"But if the collector only wanted it for his own personal use, that would not matter."

"True," said Budge. A worried look began to spread over his countenance. "I just hope the mummy hasn't been ground down into powder and sold as medicine," he said.

"If that were the objective I doubt if the perpetrators would bother going to all the trouble of procuring the mummy of a priest," said Holmes. "Any old mummy would do."

"True again," said Budge. "In that case, I am at my wits' end."

"Fortunately, I am only at the beginning of mine," said Holmes.

It was still daylight when we reached the museum. All the visitors had gone and the iron gates were locked. Budge produced a key. He led us round the impressive Doric building to an entrance at the back. We had to walk quite fast to keep up with him. We went up several staircases until we came to the corridor which he had mentioned, and continued on towards the door where the antiquities were kept. A guard was on duty there. "Is this the same guard as the one to which you were referring?" asked Holmes as we approached.

"Yes," said Budge. The guard appeared startled when we made our presence known.

"I hear you had rather an unsettling experience a few nights ago," said Holmes.

The guard stared at Holmes in alarm.

"I'm sorry, allow me to introduce myself. I am Sherlock Holmes, Consulting Detective," said Holmes, offering his card. The guard took it, still in the same glazed manner.

"Sherlock Holmes," he said in a vernacular as he took the card. "The Great Detective."

"I am gratified that you appear to know my name," said Holmes. "If you could just tell me in your own words exactly what happened on that night."

"Well, I were sitting here, as usual, and as usual, nothing were 'appening. I took a glance at my pocket watch and it were near three o'clock. I went to the lavatory, then returned to my post. It was then that I noticed that the door to this room were very slightly open."

"Continue," said Holmes.

"Well, it were just then that I thought I could see a man all bandaged up from head to foot, strolling away down the far end of the corridor. He was only there for a few seconds then he disappeared around the corner. There ain't nothing wrong with my eyesight, Governor, especially long distance."

"Are you sure you were awake?"

"At that moment, yes. I know when I'm awake and when I'm asleep."

A dignified, middle-aged, affluent sort of man was approaching from the far end of the corridor. "Ah, hello, Budge," he said as he came up to us. "Who are these people?"

"This is Mr. Holmes, a consulting detective, and his friend and colleague, Dr. Watson. They are assisting me in my investigations."

"Are they? Jolly good," said the affable man whom I surmised was a director of the museum.

"Mr. Garger was just telling us about the apparition that he witnessed," said Budge.

"Ah, yes," said the director. "I have just had information that one of the other night guards also claims he saw it."

"Really?" I said, in surprise. But the director was now walking away along the corridor.

Budge unlocked the door to the chamber. "Step this way, Mr. Holmes," he said. We went into a room with high windows that were barred from top to bottom.

"It must be clear to anyone outside the building that this room holds something of value," said Holmes.

"Yes, I suppose it is," said Budge. "This is the only room on the upper floors of the building with barred windows."

A long, wooden table was positioned in the middle of the room upon which lay two wooden sarcophagi, decorated with painted birds and hieroglyphics.

"The one on the right is of Ankhefenkhons," said Budge. "The one on the left, Nesperennub. We have opened both sarcophagi; however we did not unseal the cartonnage cases containing the mummies. The cartonnage case of Ankhefenkhons has been broken open." To demonstrate, he lifted the uppermost part of the sarcophagus of Ankhefenkhons to reveal a second painted case within, split into two pieces.

"And you are sure that the mummy was inside this cartonnage case twenty-four hours ago?"

"Oh, yes, most definitely. We had no intention of unsealing the cartonnage cases, for advanced technologies are imminent that will enable us to examine the mummies without unwrapping them. We wish to preserve the mummies until these technologies are available."

"Do you mean X-rays?" I asked.

"That is correct," said Budge. "These are exciting times for Egyptologists."

"Which are the safes that hold the other artefacts?" asked Holmes.

"Over here," said Budge, indicating a row of safes on a wall. "Nothing has been taken, but the dials have been moved. Fortunately, we use the most up-to-date safe security available."

"So it would appear that if the mummy did indeed break out of his cartonnage case, he then attempted to open the safes. No, I think it is more probable that the cartonnage case was broken open by someone from the outside whose interest was not confined to the mummies."

"Why did they take only one?" I asked. "And why was the mummy seen wandering the corridors of the museum?"

"The practical difficulties of taking two may have been prohibitive," said Holmes, observing the broken cartonnage case. "As for the mummy coming to life, I doubt very much that whatever it was that the guards saw was the stolen mummy. It may have been an attempt to fuel the 'Curse of the Mummy' story. No doubt the D— has already got hold of it."

"Well, this is all very clarifying," said Budge. "But it still does not get me any further in recovering the mummy. What would you say were my chances of success?"

"I cannot say at present," said Holmes. "However, I believe the mummy is likely to be still intact, for it is the mummy of a priest and therefore of added value in its intact state."

"Well, that is good to know," said Budge, letting out a sigh. "But what I can't understand is, how did the thieves get in?"

"Not through the window," said Holmes. "It is too

high up and the bars are undisturbed. If it were thieves, they came through the door. There is no sign that the lock has been tampered with, so I would deduce that whoever it was must have had a key."

"A key?" exclaimed Budge. "Only a very few members of staff have a key."

"Well, whoever took the mummy also did," said Holmes. "Is there anyone on your list of staff members who has only recently started working here?"

"Well, of course, there are the guards," said Budge. "They come and go all the time. The only person I can really think of is my own personal assistant Adofo, who came back with me from Egypt. However, I did not give him a key and my own key to this room is constantly on my person whenever I am in the museum. At home, I keep it locked in a drawer. In any case, Adofo is above suspicion. I have never known him to be anything other than loyal and honest."

"Nevertheless," said Holmes. "I would like to talk to him."

"I am afraid he is not here," said Budge. "He went back to Egypt a few days ago."

"When will he return?"

"I do not expect him to return. He is now assistant to the director of the Egyptian Museum in Giza, a position that will soon become permanent."

"Interesting," said Holmes. "Have you ever met the director of this museum?"

"I have," said Budge. "Our meeting was a short one. He accused me of being a thief. I told him that as long as Egypt continued to treat its antiquities in such a careless manner, it was not theft but preservation."

"When is your next trip to Egypt scheduled for?"

"Well, it was scheduled for now; I was hoping to do some research in the archives where papyri found during excavations have been placed. But then this business with the mummy came up and I have had to postpone the trip."

"Where did Adofo live during his time in London?" continued Holmes.

"He did not tell me," said Budge. "But I think he once mentioned the London Docks."

"There are virtually no Egyptians in London," said Holmes. "They prefer to stay in their own country, even at times of poverty. He would have stood out. Would you have a photograph of him?"

"Why, yes, said Budge. "There is one taken at an excavation in Egypt at which he was present. It is in another office. I shall get it for you. I cannot, however, leave you alone in this room, as I hope you will understand."

"If I could borrow it for a couple of days that would be useful. And now, with your permission I shall conduct a thorough examination of this room."

"By all means, Mr. Holmes," said Budge. Holmes got out his glass and went systematically over the walls, floor and contents. However, he did not seem to find anything.

"Here is the photograph," said Budge, as we stood in his office. "Adofo is the one on the far right."

"Thank you," said Holmes, taking a brief glance before pocketing it.

"Do you have a plan, Mr. Holmes?" asked Budge.

"I have an area of investigation on which to focus," answered Holmes. "However, I can apply my methods to it better if I work alone. When I have made further progress I will report back to you by telegram."

With this assurance we departed from the museum. Budge let us out of the gates and we took a hansom back to Baker Street.

"Will you be requiring my assistance in your further investigation?" I enquired as we rattled along Tottenham Court Road.

"I shall be working undercover," said Holmes. "And that always works best if I am alone. Hopefully I shall be better informed of the facts of the case by tomorrow evening."

I awoke early the following morning. Unable to sleep I emerged from my bedchamber into the sitting room, where I was surprised to find a shabby, half-drunken sailor, standing in the middle of the room.

"Are you here to see Mr. Holmes?" I asked, calmly.

"That's right," said the weather-worn man, turning towards me. "Only he ain't 'ere. And now, Watson, I have to go out. I shall be in the vicinity of the London Docks."

"If you have not returned by this evening I shall head straight down there," I said. I vaguely recollected having seen Holmes as a sailor some time before.

Holmes walked off in the direction of the Metropolitan station, leaving me to contemplate on what his intentions might be. Mrs. Hudson came into the sitting-room and began laying out the breakfast things. I sat down, poured myself coffee, and picked up the copy of The Times that she had brought up. Outside in the street a paper-boy was selling the D——. The devil in me made me pull up the window to hear what he was shouting.

"'Mummy' Wanders Corridors of British Museum," he was urgently repeating. I tossed a ha'penny down to him and he swung up a copy to me. I pulled down the window again and sat down to read.

Last Thursday at about three o'clock in the morning, a night-guard in the British Museum reports he observed a bandaged figure walking along the far end of a corridor on one of the upper floors. This coincided remarkably with the disappearance of an Ancient Egyptian mummy from the room outside which the guard was posted. The bandaged figure was also observed by a second guard on the landing of the floor below. The directors of the museum are anxious to recover the mummy, which was that of a priest by name of Ankhefenkhons, and are considering offering a reward for its return in an intact state. No other artefacts are known to have been taken on this night; however, thefts of valuable objects from the British Museum are not unknown.

The Arabs of the first century believed that whoever disturbed the tomb of an Ancient Egyptian would be placed under a curse, and that the mummy of the Ancient Egyptian whose tomb has been disturbed would come back to life. This belief is still held today by many people all over the world. However, Sir Henry Ratton, writer and biographer, condemns such a belief, for it 'promotes the superstitious trend that has gained such momentum in recent years.'

I considered that there would be more visitors to the British Museum as a result of this story. In fact, with such publicity the museum was probably financially better off than it had been before the mummy was stolen.

I cannot say that I made myself particularly useful over the coming few hours. Holmes had taken over the case and I thought it best to wait until he had something to report. I have on occasion, acted on my own initiative and it proved in most cases to be a mistake. When he finally did return, he had dropped the 'sailor act' and walked in simply as himself, made-up as a sailor.

"Well?" I enquired.

Holmes retreated into his room and emerged a couple of minutes later. I was always amazed at how quickly he discarded his veneer. He immediately lit his black clay pipe and sat down in his velvet armchair.

"I have found the lodging house where Adofo had diggings," he said, between puffs of smoke. "He shared a room there with two other Egyptians. However, they all left a few days ago. The landlord allowed me to take a look at their room for I told him I was interested in renting it myself. It looked out onto the water. I found nothing there, save a couple of cigar ends of an Egyptian variety. On further investigation a little way up the river I discovered that the Egyptians had hired a steamboat a few days ago from a boat owner who told me they had taken it out all the way along the Thames Estuary, where they had eventually met up with a ship, which they had boarded. Their luggage had consisted of a rectangular box which was taken onto the ship."

"Where was the ship heading for?" I asked.

"The steam-boat owner said he did not know. It had no flag. The name of the ship was not visible."

"Well, if I am not very much mistaken, that ship was

bound for Egypt," I said. "And the box contained the stolen mummy."

"Very good, Watson," said Holmes. "There is much circumstantial evidence to support that theory. And circumstantial evidence is all we have to go on, right now."

"We have not fulfilled our mission to recover the mummy," I said. "How do you propose we do that?"

"We wait until Adofo surfaces again," said Holmes. "Ships from London to the port of Alexandria generally take about six weeks. However, this one may get there a bit faster."

At this moment, Mrs. Hudson entered the sitting-room, accompanied by what appeared to be a man of learning. It was not Budge.

"I'm sorry, Mr. Holmes," she said. "This gentleman insisted on seeing you now."

"That is quite all right, Mrs. Hudson," said Holmes. "I am always ready to receive clients."

I immediately moved from my chair opposite Holmes and invited the visitor to sit down. I then went to my writing-chair.

"Dr. Watson, I presume," said the learned man with a smile.

"That is correct," I said.

"Mr. Holmes, I am a marked man," began the visitor, without any preamble. "But first let me introduce myself. I am Arthur Steele, excavator of the tomb of Ankhefenkhons."

"The stolen mummy," said Holmes.

"That is correct," said the Egyptologist. "I perceive that you do not believe in the curse of the mummy. It might therefore surprise you to be told that last night, the mummy appeared in the hallway of my villa in Kent, returned to life."

"How did it get in?" asked Holmes.

"My servant let it in. My wife then appeared in the hallway and it advanced towards her. She was so frightened that she fainted. By the time I arrived on the scene, two more of my servants were there, attempting to restrain it. It had the strength of ten men."

"I doubt it," said Holmes. "I myself have exceptional strength; however, it would not equal that of ten men. I trust this 'mummy' did not get any farther than the hallway."

"No," said Steele. "I fired at it with my revolver. But the bullets just seem to drop off it. It eventually turned and left. Two of my servants followed it, keeping their distance. It headed for the marshlands, where it disappeared into the fog."

"Have you informed the police?" enquired Holmes.

"No," I said. "I would lose my reputation overnight, were I to report such a thing. That is why I have come to you."

"You fear that the mummy will return?"

"Not necessarily. However, I feel that I am next on the list of those under the curse of the mummy."

"In which you believe."

"No. But I cannot ignore statistics. Since the opening of the tomb of Ankhefenkhons there have been no less than twenty-one untimely deaths of those involved in its opening. The most recent was that of my assistant, who fell from a hotel balcony in the most suspect of circumstances. Another was shot dead, allegedly by his wife in the Savoy. A third was found smothered at his club in Mayfair."

"Have there been any others in London?" asked Holmes.

"No," said Steele. "The rest died of a feverish condition in Egypt."

"How long ago was it that you arrived back in England?"

"About a month ago."

"Then it would appear that you will not succumb to whatever it was that killed at most eighteen Egyptologists in Egypt."

"I would agree with that. However, now that I am in London, I feel that I am in danger more than ever before."

"What is the name of this club in which your fellow Egyptologist was found dead?"

"The Osiris Club. It is frequented mainly by intellectuals with an unhealthy interest in occultism."

"I take it you are not a member of this club."

"No. But I believe that one of my fellow Egyptologists is. Fellow or rival, depending on how you look at it. He is known to dabble in the occult."

"His name?"

"Wallis Budge. He has a position at the British Museum."

"Thank you, Mr. Steele," said Holmes. "That is most enlightening. As for you, it would appear that you are safer in Egypt than in London. I would suggest that you return there, until this matter is resolved."

"Sixteen Egyptologists met with sudden death there," Steele reminded Holmes.

"But all of them with a fever. As long as you do not contract such a thing from a tomb or otherwise, you should survive."

"I may take your advice, Mr. Holmes," said Steele. "I spend half the year in Egypt as it is. It should not take long to make the arrangements. Do you have anything more to add?"

"I shall endeavour to find out who or what is behind the curse of the mummy, said Holmes. "It may be that there is nothing behind it. However, the matter is worthy of further investigation."

"Then I shall leave you now, Mr. Holmes," said the visitor. "Please inform me as soon as you have any news."

Mr. Steele rose from the chair in which he had been sitting, bowed slightly to me and Holmes, and left.

"You really think there is something in this 'Curse of the Mummy' story?" I asked, incredulously.

"Most probably. However, I do not believe it to be of a supernatural nature. We have made great progress as a result of this interview with Mr. Steele. He has saved me a lot of footwork."

"Really?" I said.

"I will send a telegram to Budge asking him to return at his earliest convenience," said Holmes. He went over to his desk and began to write quickly. Then he opened the door to the room. "Billy!" he called out. The pageboy was never far away. He came up directly.

"Take this to the post office immediately," he said.

Holmes closed the door again.

"No doubt Budge will be here again in no time," he said, sitting down by the fireplace again.

Budge wasted no time in responding. He was back on our premises within a couple of hours.

"You have news, Mr. Holmes?" he said, as soon as he entered the sitting-room.

"Yes," said Holmes. "I have not been able to recover the mummy. However, I have an idea as to where it might be." He began to explain his finding of that morning.

"So you see, Mr. Budge, the mummy is most likely winging its way back to Alexandria at this very moment," he said.

"It must be confiscated at the port in Egypt," said Budge. "For it is now the property of the British."

"And how will you prove that?" enquired Holmes.

"There will be an amulet or something of that nature, attached to the inner wrappings of the mummy."

"Which you cannot access without removing the outer wrappings, thereby destroying the mummy. When it reaches the Egyptian Museum, it will be exhibited in a new cartonnage case and given a new identity," went on Holmes. "However, there will be those who have knowledge of its true identity. After a while this knowledge will become a rumour, then a myth. Unless you can identify a mummy from its wrappings I am very much afraid that you will have to let the matter go."

"You do not appear to be motivated in getting it back," said Budge. "In time there will exist the means to examine the mummy in a scientific manner as never before. If the British Museum could just keep it until then …"

"In time, science may be able to identify the mummy as the one stolen from the British Museum. You will then be able to claim it back; that is, assuming the law has not changed by then."

Budge sighed.

"Have you any idea what will happen to that mummy if it is left in Egypt?" he said. "The way they treat their relics, it will be lucky to last six months. If kept in the British Museum, it will last centuries, if not millennia."

"If it had been left in the ground in the first place, it would have been preserved pretty well, I should think."

"We can discover no new knowledge from a mummy left in the ground," said Budge. "However, I see no point in continuing this conversation. At least you have given me an excuse to travel to Egypt again. I shall inform the Museum that the mummy is most likely located in the Egyptian Museum, giving your reasons. I shall endeavour to get it back on my own initiative. I have learnt something of your methods over the past few days. Name your fee and I shall be gone."

"I require no fee," said Holmes. "However, if you are able to supply it, I would like some information."

"What information?"

"I believe that you are a member of the Osiris Club, in Mayfair. It is very possible that one of your associates there is behind this whole mummy business. If you could give me a list of names ..."

"No, I could not," said Budge. "The membership list of the club is kept secret. I don't know how you found out that I am a member."

"When did you last visit the club?"

"A week ago last Saturday."

"Please tell me exactly what happened that evening."

"Well, I arrived about eight p.m., spoke to a couple of people and went home a few hours later."

"You go too fast," said Holmes. "Please give me as much detail as you feel that you are able."

"All right," said Budge. "I arrived at the club. I stepped in through the revolving door. It was exactly four minutes to eight, according to the clock in the hallway. I went up to the porter's lodge where I deposited my greatcoat. I was in evening dress. I signed the members' book then entered the members' lounge, which lies to the left of the porter's lodge. Inside, I met a member who is frequently there; however, I cannot give you his name. After about half-an-hour, the member left. I spoke to a couple of others at length inside the lounge. At a quarter to midnight, I took part in what I will describe to you as a séance. This took place in another room. Around one thirty in the morning, I went home."

"When you left, I presume you collected your greatcoat from the porter's lodge."

"I did."

"And it was, I presume, present and correct. No items taken from its pockets?"

"No. My keys and revolver were both there."

"You then went home and locked the keys into a drawer, as usual?"

"Yes."

"Well, I think that is all I need to know. I am sorry not to have been of further assistance in recovering the mummy, but I believe the matter is now out of my hands."

"You have been of considerable help to me," said Budge. "I will inform you by letter of whatever transpires in Egypt."

"Is that really the end of the matter?" I asked of Holmes, after our second Egyptologist for the day had left.

"Not at all," said Holmes. "We must act fast. We shall go down to the Osiris Club directly after dinner. As gentlemen of sorts, we will not look amiss. You will distract the porter, whilst I take a look at the members' book."

"How will I do that?"

Holmes looked at his watch.

"You have exactly one hour to think of something, Watson," he said. "I shall be relying on you."

The Osiris Club was tucked away in a side street off Piccadilly. Two Egyptian statues flanked the entrance; there was no sign. We stepped in through the revolving door as Budge had described. There was no one in the hallway; presumably it was too early for Osiris members. We went up to the porter's lodge, whereupon I began to walk off along the corridor.

"Excuse me, sir, are you a member?" I heard the porter calling out.

"Is he ...?" The porter emerged from his cubicle and hurried after me. I had already rounded the corner when he caught up with me. I stopped and turned round.

"Sir, if you are not a member you cannot wander freely around the place. This is not a public building."

"Is it not? I could have sworn it was," I said. "I was looking for the restaurant."

"The restaurant is not open until eight, sir. And it is open only to members. If you will step this way, sir." The dutiful and arrogant porter attempted to jostle me back along the corridor.

"Now look here, my man," I said. "You clearly do not know who I am. Please refrain from touching my person."

"I'm sorry, sir," said the porter, backing off. "It's just that I have been instructed not to let anyone in who isn't a member."

"I am soon to be a member," I said. "And when I am, I will have a word with your superior. You do not appear to know your place. Your name, if you please."

"Oh, sir," said the porter, with pitiful chagrin.

"Never mind. I shall find out anyway, in due course. Now, if you would be so good as to direct me to the restaurant, so that I may find it in future."

"This way, sir," said the porter, nervously and uncertainly. When he had done so, I felt I could not distract him any longer. I returned to the entrance hallway; Holmes was nowhere to be seen. I left the premises and found him lounging outside, smoking a cigarette. We immediately walked off together.

"I did not find that an altogether pleasant experience," I reprimanded Holmes as we walked back along Piccadilly in search of a cab. "In future, I would prefer it if you were the decoy."

"You did marvellously," said Holmes. "Within the short period of time that you were able to detain that prig of a porter, I obtained all the information I needed. On Saturday, 9th September, a member whose name appears frequently in the members' book arrived at the club a little before Budge. His name is Harold Riley; no doubt he is listed in my index."

"I am surprised how little space your index takes up," I said when we were back in Baker Street. "Considering that it appears to contain the names of half the known world."

"Here we are," said Holmes. "Harold Riley. Occultist and Satanist. Born into an upper class family in 1865. Member of the Hermetic Order of the Golden Dawn. Known to experience the symptoms of dementia praecox, he is rumoured to have murdered his servants in India. Believes himself to be a prophet of a new age of personal liberty, controlled by the ancient Egyptian god Horus. Heavyweight boxer and accomplished swordsman. How is that for a suspect, Watson?"

"How is this man linked to the disappearance of the mummy?" I asked.

"Circumstantial evidence links him to that event and the events surrounding it. He is therefore a suspect. The evidence is this: One: he had the opportunity to borrow from Budge's greatcoat the key to the room where the mummy was kept, and could therefore have made a copy. Two: As a heavyweight boxer, he would have the same build as the phantom 'mummy' that has been terrorising London these past few days. Three: from his beliefs and practices it is likely that he would object strongly to the desecration of Ancient Egyptian tombs. Four: He is acquainted with Budge and therefore has a link to Adofo, who may have stolen the mummy. Five: he is rumoured to be homicidal. Six: a man involved in the desecration of the tomb of Ankhefenkhons was found murdered at the Osiris Club."

"But as you said, Holmes, it is all circumstantial. How will you find conclusive evidence?"

"I shall ask Gregson to put a watch on him," said Holmes. "I do not have the facilities to observe Riley twenty-four hours a day. And Gregson is not averse to breaking the law occasionally, should the ends be justified."

"Will Gregson listen?"

"Gregson was on the scene after Steele's assistant fell to his death from a hotel balcony. The verdict at the inquest was suicide; however, Gregson may not have been entirely convinced. He is the smartest of the Scotland Yarders. I have been of assistance to him on several occasions and will welcome the information that I shall impart to him."

"But if Riley is innocent ..."

"Then I have pursued an innocent man. However, if, as I suspect, he is behind the 'curse of the mummy' phenomenon, the lives of the remaining tomb desecrators may be saved, including that of Budge."

"One thing I can't understand, Holmes," I ventured. "How is it that the bullets dropped off the mummy in Arthur Steele's villa? He said he shot at it."

"A bulletproof vest, most likely, Watson," said Holmes.

It was less than a fortnight later, into the month of October that I was once again reading the D—. The 'Curse of the Mummy' had ceased to be headline news and the event in Arthur Steele's villa had never made it into any of its columns. I was therefore startled by a sensational account of the latest developments concerning the mummy, of which I had not yet been told first hand.

"Are you aware that the mummy has now been arrested?" I enquired of Holmes, as he sat at his laboratory.

"Gregson is yet to inform me of that," said Holmes. "Be so good as to read the article to me."

"Certainly," I said, turning towards him.

'MUMMY' APPREHENDED

Thanks to the quick action of Inspector Gregson of Scotland Yard, the 'mummy' who has been creating havoc all around London this past week is now behind bars. At about a quarter to eleven last night, following reports of a 'mummy' breaking into the premises of Lord Westhill, sponsor to a renowned Egyptologist, a figure bandaged from head to foot was seen from the window of a neighbouring house, letting himself into the back entrance of the home of Harold Riley. Police who were watching the house immediately moved in and apprehended it. With half of its bandages removed, the figure was found to be Riley himself. Upon questioning, he made no secret of his doings, saying that those who would desecrate the tomb of Ankhefenkhons could expect to incur the wrath of the mummy. He is being questioned in relation to his possible involvement in the recent deaths of several Egyptologists in London, which are now being regarded as suspect. Police have seized Riley's diaries and books, all of which indicate an obsessive interest in Ancient Egyptian mysticism, and a deranged mind.

"Will you never take credit yourself, Holmes?" I asked, wearily. "I know you say that your work is its own reward, but to give the likes of Lestrade, Gregson and Bradstreet so much undue credit is surely wrong."

"Not at all," said Holmes. "All the aforementioned police detectives are in dire need of undue credit. I myself need none; my reputation suffices. Were Gregson and Co. not employed by the police force, they would be unable to find work, whereas I, with the exception of a few short, dry periods, have more than I am able to take on. And that," said Holmes, as the bell downstairs rang out clearly and definitively, "I believe is a client."

The Vicar's Note

Although Holmes has been known to say that his work is its own reward, he is not averse to accepting remuneration from affluent clients in excess of his usual fees. The King of Bohemia and the French Republic are but two examples. These alone increased his wealth by such an extent that had he so wished, he could now have lived in a quiet fashion, devoting all his time to chemical researches. Other clients have also served to fulfil that purpose albeit to a lesser extent. In the case that I am about to relate, it was clear from the start that such a client was involved. It was of an afternoon in October 1882 that the holder of a baronetcy in the vicinity of Knaresborough called in on Holmes without an appointment. He was not reticent as to his social standing but immediately introduced himself as Sir John Rakestraw, eighth Baronet. Having thus clarified his identity, he was invited by Holmes to sit down.

"I am in London on business," said the baronet. "And thought I might take the opportunity of calling on you, in the hope that you would clear up a matter that has been pre-occupying me these last few days."

"I shall endeavour to do so," said Holmes. "You have

come from the headquarters of Collis' Bank."

"Absolutely right," said John Rakestraw. "If I did not know better, I would say that you were psychic. As a matter of fact, the issue upon which I wish to speak to you is related to clairvoyance. But first, tell me how you obtained this information. I would like to become knowledgeable of your methods."

"There is mud at the end of your trousers of a bluish tint," said Holmes. "Owing to the road works currently taking place around the building of that bank. The clay underlying that area is peculiar in that it contains mineral deposits that cause it to appear blue."

"It is amazing what can be deduced from little information," said the baronet. "A clear demonstration of your methods. You probably think that you are unique, Mr. Holmes. Well, I can tell you that you are not; you have a match in the form of a woman, currently residing at the village inn, not two miles from my house. She took a room there a couple of weeks ago, claiming to be a descendant of Mother Shipton. She cannot read or write, but has greatly impressed the villagers with her clairvoyant abilities. Not only that, she has been taking money off them. My own groom, for example, had a wager with her at the inn on the evening that she arrived, which he lost. It was an even-money bet that two of the people present in the room in which they sat would have the same birthday. I can understand why he took on the wager. There are three hundred and sixty-five days in a year, and there were only about fifty people in the room. He went round and asked everyone for their birthday. It turned out that the woman was right. I cannot think how she knew. It would be very troublesome to find out the birthday of everyone in the village. Perhaps she was just lucky."

"She was certainly not unlucky," said Holmes.

"No. The woman then proceeded to guess the line of work of everyone in the room. Ninety per cent of the time, she guessed right."

"I doubt that she was guessing," said Holmes.

"I am inclined to agree," said the baronet. "Then a few days later, having heard of the woman's extraordinary capacity, the landlady asked her if she could do a reading for her. The woman, who goes by the name of Miss Sondheil, consented. Miss Sondheil lay down upon the sofa in the sitting-room and went into a state of self-induced hypnosis. In this trance she gave an accurate description of the landlady's childhood, including details of her innermost thoughts at the time. When the woman emerged from the trance, she could remember nothing about it. From then on, the landlady has warmed to the woman, allowing her to stay at the inn free of charge, meals included."

A look of amusement crossed over Holmes' countenance.

"How long has the landlady lived at the inn?" he enquired.

"Oh, as long as I can remember," replied the baronet. "I think she has always lived there."

"It is as I would expect," said Holmes.

"What would you expect?"

"Oh, no matter," said Holmes. "You are of the opinion that the woman is a charlatan?"

"Indeed I am," said the baronet. "I believe that she is not clairvoyant at all, but is using the very same methods as you do. It works on the villagers but it does not work on me. I was hoping that you might be able to tell me how she is achieving her results."

"Why is it of any interest to you?" asked Holmes. "She could be regarded as an entertainer of sorts."

"The parson has come to me, complaining that his congregation is falling," said the baronet. "Not that that is of any interest to me, either. I would have paid little attention to the woman, were it not for the fact that she has now made a prediction concerning me." The baronet paused, as though considering the enormity of the situation.

"I take it that it was not a welcome prediction," said Holmes, finally.

"It was about the worst prediction that she could have made. She said that I would become a pauper within a year."

Holmes appeared to be trying not to snigger. The baronet observed him unsmilingly. "I sense that you do not defer to your betters in the manner that is expected of you," he said. "You are entitled to your views, whatever they are. However, I would appreciate it if for the time being, you were to take this matter seriously."

"Oh, I do," said Holmes. "It is indeed a terrible prediction, for pauperism is something that you have doubtless never known. I shall endeavour to get to the bottom of this as soon as possible."

"Thank you, Mr. Holmes," said the baronet. "I would be enormously grateful if you would."

With this indication that there was money in the case, Holmes sat up in his armchair, a look of concentrated eagerness pervading his strong features. "Under what circumstances was this prediction concerning your future financial situation made?" he enquired.

"It came straight from the woman herself. She had come to my house and had gone round to the back entrance, presenting herself to my servants as a fortune-teller. I happened to be arriving when she left, and recognized her as the woman at the inn. Still on my horse, I went over to her, to find out what she might be doing on my property. She said to me, "You may ride high now but shall be a pauper within a year." Normally, I would dismiss this as nonsensical gibberish, but as virtually all the predictions that she has made have come true, I find myself unable to do so. Though I cannot think how it could be possible; I own land and property; I do not gamble; I have given my wife no grounds for divorce."

"All of which the woman is probably aware. There may be more to know about you than you know yourself."

"I have thought of that," said the baronet. "Which only serves to aggravate my anxiety."

"I feel a visit to the village may be in order," said Holmes. "In order to investigate the case more fully."

"Well, if it would help, I could put you up in my manor for any length of time," said the baronet.

"That is most hospitable of you," said Holmes. "However, I feel that we might discover more were we to reside at the village inn. I trust the woman is still there?"

"Oh, yes. She has made herself very comfortable and is showing no signs of leaving."

"Then we shall travel up there as gentleman upon a genealogical quest. We shall inquire of the local history and consult the parish records; that will give me a chance to talk to the parson as well. As far as everyone in the village is concerned, we have never met the eighth Baronet Rakestraw. Have you told anyone of your visit here?"

"No one. It was only today that I had the idea of consulting you."

"Then we shall arrive in a couple of days. I have no doubt that I can unravel this matter for you."

"Do you have a theory, Mr. Holmes?"

"I have several theories. However, a lack of data prevents me from favouring one above the other. When I have more information, I shall present you with a possible theory; with any luck, it will be the only possible theory."

"That is satisfactory for the time being," said the baronet, getting up to leave. "I look forward to 'making the acquaintance' of you two gentleman in my native environment." With a hopeful spring in his step, he left our sitting-room and descended the stairs in a stately tread.

"You must be looking forward to meeting this woman, Holmes," I said, when he had gone. "If she really is your counterpart."

"The means may be the same but the ends are different," said Holmes, going over to his room. "I shall take care that she does not see through me. Remember, Watson, that we shall be travelling in the capacity of gentlemen, not detectives. Our clothes must reflect our social status; I would suggest that you hire a wardrobe."

"If you so wish. What name shall I take?"

"Bannerman," said Holmes. "And I shall be Fortescue."

*

It was not twenty-four hours before we found ourselves in the caverns of York station, clambering aboard a train to Knaresborough. The train chugged off almost as soon as I had closed the door. We passed by the backs of terraced houses and then, as the landscape opened up into green fields, Holmes got out a pamphlet describing the highlights of Knaresborough, which he began to read.

"It would appear that the person of greatest significance in this region is the prophetess Ursula Sondheil, better known as Mother Shipton. She is reputed to have been born in a cave in Knaresborough in 1488 and wrote prophetic verses. I believe this woman is very popular throughout England at the moment, Watson. Did she not write a verse to the effect that the end of the world was last year? It ran something like:

The world to an end shall come
In eighteen hundred and eighty-one

"She probably did not write that verse," I said. "I have heard that many of her so called verses are fake. That does not mean that she was not a real prophetess of her time."

"Our mystery woman claims to be her descendant," said Holmes. "And she does have the name of Sondheil; however, this may be an assumed name. If and when we meet her, it might be better not to show scepticism. Everything will become clear in due course."

It was but sixteen miles to Knaresborough and hardly any time before we were there. A trap was waiting outside the station, whose service we immediately accepted. Holmes gave the name of the inn and the village; the trap took off through the cobbled streets of the ancient market town and out along the river, passing underneath the impressive viaduct. As we travelled on, the ruins of Knaresborough Castle became visible in the landscape beyond. The village was not two miles away. At its edge lay the old coaching inn with bay windows, a red-tiled roof and a cosy interior with brick walls and ancient oak beams. It had been neglected since the coaching era and was in need of renovation; however, they had the rooms that we needed, and we were shown them without question. I wondered if lunch was being served.

"It is still early," said Holmes. "We should go out to the parish church and began our investigations straight away. What do you say, Watson?"

"We shall be back in very good time for dinner, I trust," I said.

The parish church was not situated within the village but was a mile to the north. The road was still much in the same state as it had been for the last two hundred years. Holmes immediately began to stride off along it, ignoring the mud. As we went along, we had only the sheep for company, bleating disrespectfully in the open, grassy spaces. When we got to the wall that encircled the church, there were sheep grazing in such close proximity that they could have walked into the building. We came in through the lych-gate and went up the path that led up to a heavy door. It was dim and musty inside the church. At first, we thought there to be no one around, but then the vicar appeared out of nowhere, attired in his vestments.

"May I help you?" he enquired, in the friendliest of tones.

"Good afternoon, Vicar," said Holmes. "My name

is Fortescue, and this is my friend and colleague, Bannerman. We are currently staying at the village inn and are most eager to trace our ancestors who came from this area. We were wondering if we might consult the parish records."

"That's strange," said the parson. "You are the second person this week to ask for those records. The first was Miss Sondheil, whom you may have met. I believe she is also residing at the inn."

"So we have been told," said Holmes. "However, we have not yet had the pleasure of meeting her. She sounds like quite a character."

"Indeed," said the parson. "A dangerous and independent woman, I would say. I shall be glad to see the back of her if the truth be told."

"And you say she came here to consult the parish records," said Holmes. "I was under the impression from the villagers that she could not read or write."

"She cannot," replied the vicar. "I was obliged to help her. I was not prepared to sift through three hundred years of records; however I did show her how the names of 'Sondheil' and 'Shipton' are written, so that she might conduct the search herself. She sat at that table over there with the books for over an hour, but found nothing."

I glanced over to where a room accessed by a few steps was half-hidden by curtains. Inside was a long table, upon which lay a number of large, heavy, black books in two piles.

"May we have a look ourselves?" asked Holmes.

"By all means," said the vicar. "The ones on the table are all late seventeenth, early eighteenth century. If you require any others, I should be able to bring them out for you. The records for this parish go back as far as the sixteenth century."

"Thank you," said Holmes. "These will do for the moment." We went over to the table and sat down. An arch window illuminated the surroundings.

"I believe we shall find something of significance somewhere within this data," said Holmes, opening the book at the top of one of the piles. "Though it may take some time."

"What are we looking for, exactly?" I asked.

"References to the Rakestraw Baronets," said Holmes. "The woman may have discovered something amongst these records to their detriment."

"The Rakestraw Baronets," I repeated, taking the book that lay at the top of the other pile and opening it. A cloud of invisible dust immediately pervaded the atmosphere. With the utmost care, I turned to the first page. It displayed a list of marriages written in copybook handwriting, dating from June, 1666. Someone had at one time been through it, crossing off the entries in pencil. As I skimmed down the rows, I could find nothing that referred to a member of the baronet's family, bar one virtually illegible note in the margin, written all those years ago. I could just about make out the name, 'Rakestraw'.

"What about this, Holmes?" I asked. "I can't read it."

Holmes immediately took the volume from me.

"Prayers given for the safe return of Captain Sir Josiah Rakestraw, first Bt, who has long since been away in the war against Holland. Excellent work, Watson. I believe we now hold the key to solving the problem that we have been assigned."

"Already?" I said. "I don't see how."

"If the first baronet was away in wars on the 17th July, 1667 then he could not have been here," said Holmes. "It is as I suspected. A case of illegitimacy."

"What do you mean, Holmes?"

Holmes put down the volume open on the table and picked up the one that he had previously been consulting. He opened it at a page near the beginning.

"John Henry Rakestraw, the second baronet, was born on 2nd April, 1668," said Holmes. "And baptised on 28th April of that year." I observed the record that Holmes was indicating. The writing was clear and distinct.

"His father, however, was away fighting the Dutch in June and July 1667," went on Holmes. "What does that tell you?"

"That the child was born late or prematurely," I said.

"Quite so, Watson. Either that or the child was illegitimate."

"Is it not odd that the birth was recorded as well as the baptism? That is not the case with any of the other entries."

"I would agree," said Holmes.

"Perhaps the birth of a baronet was more likely to be recorded than that of a villager," I suggested.

"Possibly."

"Shall I continue to search through these records?"

"No, I think we have already enough information to work on," said Holmes, closing the volumes and putting them back on the piles. "We can always return, if there is more to know." We got up and went back into the nave of the church. The vicar came over to us.

"Did you find what you were looking for?" he asked.

"Yes," said Holmes. "And far quicker than expected."

"You had more luck than Miss Sondheil, then," said the vicar. "Have you finished with the records? I really should be putting them back in the vestry."

"Yes," said Holmes. "Thank you very much for your assistance. By the way, how did your wife take to Miss Sondheil?"

"She did not," said the vicar. "Which is unusual, for my wife takes to most people. She offered to teach her to read. But the woman said that education would interfere with her psychic abilities and so she would decline. My wife told her not to indulge in such wicked nonsense and the woman left in a hurry. They have not met since."

"Well, no doubt we shall see you as we go around," said Holmes, and we left the church, stepping out into the late autumn sunshine.

"I suggest we return to the inn," said Holmes. This I welcomed, for I was hungry. To my relief, when we arrived back, Holmes requested a table in the dining room.

"Has Miss Sondheil returned?" he enquired in a casual manner.

"She has. And she has left," said the landlord. He took us over to a table covered with an indifferent tablecloth and laid with pewter crockery. We sat down at the rough, wooden benches beside it.

"Left? You mean, permanently?"

"I certainly hope so," said the landlord, pouring some wine into the goblets from a jug. He then went away.

A cheery candlelight lit up our surroundings. My mood immediately improved, as did that of Holmes, as his relaxed manner would indicate.

"So we shall not be meeting your double in the form of a woman after all," I said.

"I suspected as much," said Holmes. "Our arrival has evidently scared her away."

"But we are here as gentlemen, not detectives," I said.

"Nevertheless, we have aroused her suspicions. It is not usual for gentlemen to pass through this village. She will be far away in another village by now, no doubt claiming ancestry there as well."

"If she persists in such doings, she will soon become notorious," I said.

"She has the whole world at her disposal," said Holmes. "It will be a while before news of her reaches the outermost regions of our empire."

"What is our next move, Holmes?" I asked.

"We shall pay a visit to the baronet tomorrow morning," said Holmes. "He must be anxiously awaiting news, of which we now have plenty."

"But will he welcome the news?" I asked. "Perhaps it would be wiser not to tell him."

"We have been hired to inform him of any developments," said Holmes. "In any case, if we do not, I suspect that he will be informed by a third party in due course."

"Third party?"

"If it turns out that the second baronet was indeed illegitimate, then the rightful heir may put in a claim to his throne."

"How will he know that he is the rightful heir?"

"The woman will have told him. I have no doubt that she has read the note in the margin of the parish records."

"I thought she couldn't read."

"If you believe that, you will believe anything," said Holmes.

The baronet's house was a neat and compact pocket manor, square in design, with a walled courtyard at the front of the building. A groom hurried out to meet the hired trap in which we arrived, and a footman showed us into the entrance hall. The chequered floor was contrasted by oak panelling and bronze statues in the alcoves. The baronet himself was there to greet us.

"Mr. Holmes," he said. "I am glad that you have arrived. I trust that they have made you comfortable at the inn?"

"Very comfortable," said Holmes. "However, I can inform you amongst other things that the woman has left."

"Left?" said the baronet. "The parson will be pleased."

"We have already made the acquaintance of the Reverend Bartlett," said Holmes. "He was most helpful with our enquiries."

"You have already begun your investigation?" said the baronet in surprise.

"Oh, yes. We have all but solved the mystery."

The baronet became very serious. "Come into the drawing-room, Mr. Holmes," he said. "And you too, Dr. Watson. It is too early for whisky but perhaps a glass of champagne?" A butler appeared. "A bottle of champagne for our guests," he said. The butler disappeared again, without a word. The baronet invited us to be seated upon the red leather armchairs and sat down upon the sofa.

"Now," he said. "Let me hear your news."

"The second Baronet was likely as not, illegitimate," began Holmes without delay. "There is evidence for this in the Parish records of Knaresborough, for the years 1667 and 1668. Theoretically that would mean that you are not the rightful eighth Baronet Rakestraw."

The baronet appeared startled. "That is the worst possible news," he said. "You might have warned me." He went over to the drinks table and poured himself a glass of whisky. "How certain of this are you?"

"Not certain. As Dr. Watson pointed out, the child could have been late or premature. Did you not know of this matter?"

"I had no idea," said the baronet. "This is the first that I have heard of it. What exactly did you find in the parish records, Mr. Holmes?"

"A note in the margin, written by the vicar at the time, saying that the first baronet was away in the war against Holland about eight months before the second baronet was born."

"Could it not be a modern forgery?"

"I doubt it. The ink was faded, and there was even a line in pencil marked across it by someone at a later date."

"Has anyone else seen this note?"

"It is likely that Miss Sondheil has seen it. The book was at the top of a pile of books that she had looked through."

"Well, I am yet to receive a letter from a solicitor, informing me that my title is challenged," said the baronet. "The woman is gone now. Perhaps she will forget all about it."

"If the title is challenged, all may not be lost," said Holmes. "The evidence of the vicar's note will not, I feel, prove sufficient evidence in a court of law."

"No, but there will be plenty of other sources of evidence referring to the whereabouts of the first baronet during the crucial time period," said the eighth baronet agitatedly. "A good barrister will prove beyond reasonable doubt that the second baronet was illegitimate. I am surprised that this information is not already known."

"Have you the knowledge of who the claimant of the baronetcy would be?" enquired Holmes.

"No, I have not. No doubt he is a very common personage, with an odious occupation and a life that revolves around a five-day week."

"Have you the means to find out now his identity?"

"I expect so. However, I do not wish to."

"I admit, it may turn out to be unnecessary," said Holmes. "However, forewarned is forearmed. If a claim is put in, we shall wish to know all there is to know in advance."

"Very well," said the baronet. He got up from the sofa and went over to a fine oak cabinet, from which he took out a massive scroll of parchment. He removed the bible from the writing desk and rolled out the parchment upon it. A family tree adorned with colourful coats of arms was displayed, going back to the first Baronet Rakestraw, who purchased the manor in 1660.

"This tree is not comprehensive," he said. "However, it includes most of my not-too-distant relatives." He began to peruse the manuscript, tracing along the lines. "Despite often being away from home, the first baronet had six children," he informed us. "Three of whom were boys. So, presumably, if the first son were illegitimate, the title should by rights have gone to the second son, Godfrey, born in 1669. Now, Godfrey had three children, none of whom were boys. And so, the title would have passed back to Edgar, the third son of the first baronet." In this way, the eighth baronet pedantically worked his way down the lineage.

"That's odd," he said, finally. "It would appear that there is no heir. Take a look yourself, Mr. Holmes."

Holmes obligingly went up to the writing desk. "Unless I am very much mistaken," went on the baronet, "The legitimate male line of the Rakestraws died out in 1847. That is, assuming I am of illegitimate descent."

"There may be other male Rakestraws not mentioned on this document," said Holmes. "Otherwise, you are right. According to this tree, if the second baronet were illegitimate, there would be but one Rakestraw of legitimate descent still living – a Miss Angela Rakestraw, born 1846."

"She cannot inherit," said the baronet. "In the absence of a male heir, all that would happen is that the baronetcy would be reverted to the Crown."

"What would happen to it then?" I asked.

"The Queen would be at liberty to renew the baronetcy and bestow it upon anyone she chose."

"So, in theory, the Queen could bestow the renewed baronetcy upon Angela Rakestraw."

"An unmarried woman with no children? Not a chance," said the baronet. He rolled up the parchment again. "It would appear that the situation is not as bad as I initially thought. In the absence of a claimant, it is possible that nothing will come of this unfortunate situation. Let us drink to that." I realized that the butler was now standing in the room, holding a tray bedecked with a bottle of champagne and three crystal glasses. The baronet took the glasses and champagne from the tray and placed them upon the occasional table. "It's all right, I shall deal with it," he said. The butler duly vanished.

I have not often witnessed Holmes drinking champagne, and am not inclined to associate him with the beverage. However, on this occasion, it seemed to suit him. His eyes sparkled enigmatically as he sipped the bubbly, as though his brain were still working on the problem that had been temporarily dissolved. There was more to the matter than there appeared to be, I now realized.

"Do you intend to travel back to London, now?" asked the baronet.

"Your intoxicating Yorkshire scenery compels me to stay on a while," said Holmes. "I shall take a little holiday. However, I shall still be at your disposal, should the need arise."

"I sincerely hope that it does not," said the baronet. "It would appear that the matter can be swept back under the carpet. If you are interested in tourist attractions, I can thoroughly recommend Knaresborough Castle and the Dropping Well."

"We shall encompass both in our excursions," said Holmes, placing his champagne flute upon the coffee table. "It is all right, we can show ourselves out." Holmes and I walked back into the chequered hallway and out the heavy, oak doors into the courtyard. Our trap was brought to us immediately, harnessed with new horses and we took off to the village again.

"Are you expecting a development in this case in the near future?" I asked, as we trundled along the rough track that led across the fields to the village. The air was as good as in Switzerland and the wind as mild.

"I do not think that Miss Sondheil will waste much time," said Holmes. "She intends at the very least to wreak revenge upon the baronet, and at most, to take the baronetcy from him."

"Revenge? What has the baronet done to her? And how could she ever receive the baronetcy?"

"I have reason to believe that Miss Sondheil and Miss Angela Rakestraw are one and the same. As the last of the Rakestraws, Miss Angela Rakestraw has a tenuous claim to the baronetcy in a renewed state," said Holmes. "Were she to marry, that claim would become stronger. Children would make it stronger still. As for revenge, she has led a life of hardship whilst the eighth baronet has illicitly lived like a lord. Even if she does not benefit from the baronetcy, she would like to see him lose it."

"What shall we do for the next few days?" I enquired of Holmes.

"We are yet to learn whatever is to be learnt from the locals," said Holmes. "I suggest we take the opportunity of drinking a glass of beer with them."

With this intention in mind, a little while after arriving back at the inn Holmes and I went down from our rooms and into the tap-room. It was early afternoon and there was only one other present, whom I recognized as the groom who had taken our horses from us on our arrival at the baronet's house. He seemed an open and friendly sort of fellow who might be amenable to conversation.

"Will you take a glass of beer with us?" asked Holmes, amicably.

The groom downed what remained of his own beer and smiled across the room. "I don't mind if I do," he said, and crossed over. He was a burly sort of cove who seemed forever without trouble or strife. After Holmes had enquired of his horsey occupation and trips to the York races, the small matter of the lost wager with Miss Sondheil cropped up.

"It seemed like a good idea at the time," said the groom, woefully. "But since then, I have had an uneasy feeling that something was wrong."

"You are right to think that something was wrong," said Holmes. "When you took on that wager, there was a ninety-seven per cent chance that you would lose. Yet you only stood to double your money if you won."

"Ninety-seven per cent?" wailed the groom. "How is that possible? There were but fifty people in the room."

"You are confusing the question with another question," said Holmes. "If the question had been, what are the chances that someone in the room will have the same birthday as you do, you would indeed have been wise to take on the bet. However, that was not the question, and the two questions have two different answers, as you might expect."

"I am beginning to have an inkling of what you are saying," said the groom. "Nevertheless, I am still surprised. I shall try it out again in the next village. Only this time, I shall wager the other way. If what you are saying is true, perhaps I can make myself a living at it."

"As did Miss Sondheil," said Holmes. The groom went into a deep contemplation.

"How long have you lived here?" I asked of the groom, to break the hiatus.

"I have never been more than fifteen miles out of this village," said the groom. "I started work as a stable boy in the baronet's stables and have worked there ever since.

They are a fine family; the sixth baronet was a general and the seventh baronet was awarded the Victoria Cross during the Crimean. The second baronet was admitted to the Order of the Garter."

"What about the first baronet?" asked Holmes.

"He was the most distinguished of them all. He is said to have received the baronetcy for saving the life of Charles the Second."

"I believe he fought in a war against Holland," said Holmes.

"He fought in several. The Anglo-Dutch wars. He was a captain in the English army."

"Are there any rumours in the village of illegitimacy in the baronet's family?" asked Holmes.

The groom looked at him sharply. "You ask a lot of questions," he said. "As it happens, no. Not that I would tell you if there were."

"It would appear that the baronets were paragons of virtue," I said.

"That they were," said the groom. "I will not say a word against them."

"The baronet is lucky with his servants," said Holmes.

"The baronets have had the same servants since the baronetcy was created," said the groom. "I descend from the grooms of the previous baronets."

"Then your report of their characters is probably accurate," said Holmes.

At a quarter to three the landlady appeared. "Oh, there you are," she said cordially. "I was wondering if you two gentlemen would like to take tea in my sitting-room. I was just about to brew a pot."

"We would be most honoured," said Holmes. The groom got up to leave.

The landlady showed us into a quaint, old room with a great fireplace as centrepiece, a writing desk, and a coffee table beside which stood two high-backed, brocaded armchairs and a sofa. A bookshelf on the wall behind was stacked with inexpensive books, giving an impression of culture of some kind.

"I do not let just anyone in here," said the landlady, getting out some porcelain crockery from the cupboard in the corner. "This room is reserved for special visitors."

"We are flattered," said Holmes, sitting down in one of the armchairs. "You have some interesting books here."

"Yes," said the landlady. "I have collected them over the years. You can borrow them if you like." Lazily, Holmes picked up some of the books off the shelf and casually opened them. "I suppose Miss Sondheil was a special visitor, too," he said, finally putting the books back again.

"Oh, yes," said the landlady. "A most interesting woman."

"Did Miss Sondheil say why she was leaving in such a hurry?" asked Holmes.

A housemaid brought in an enormous copper kettle which she placed upon the coffee table. "She said that she had a sick relative in the East Riding," said the landlady. "My husband was glad to see her go. But I found her a good companion while she was here."

"Why did your husband fail to appreciate her?"

"He did not trust her. He is the most suspicious person I know. The poor woman had no money but was blessed with the gift of second sight. Only a few days after she arrived, she was able to tell me everything about my childhood that I had forgotten. Never before have I met such a sensitive spirit."

"Perhaps this might have something to do with it," said Holmes, lifting a worn notebook off the shelf. He turned to the first page covered in a block of pencilled writing and began to read:

"Sabbath morning. We set off to church in the bleary rain ..."

"That is my old diary," said the landlady. "I wrote it when I was ten."

"No doubt this is where Miss Sondheil obtained her information," said Holmes.

"That is not possible," said the landlady. "For she could not read."

"Where did you get that idea from?" asked Holmes.

"From Miss Sondheil," said the landlady. "When she arrived here, my husband requested that she sign her name in a guest book. She could hardly hold the pen, let alone write her name. In the end, she just marked the place with a cross."

"Very convincing," said Holmes.

Holmes was correct in his prediction that developments concerning the legitimacy of the baronet would soon follow. It was not ten days before a telegram from the baronet addressed to Holmes arrived at the inn, summoning him to the manor. We lost no time in heeding this request.

"The worst has occurred," said the baronet, as soon as we arrived. He showed us into his study. "I have had a letter from a solicitor informing me that if the second baronet were illegitimate, the baronetcy would now be extinct. In that case, all land and property associated with the baronetcy should have gone to Miss Rakestraw."

"Not necessarily," said Holmes. "As you told us, if the baronetcy were extinct, it could be renewed and bestowed upon another. In that case you would have to find an individual who could nominate you for it. You would then become the first baronet of the renewed baronetcy."

"But if I do not have the Rakestraw blood why should Her Majesty bestow the renewed baronetcy upon me?" objected the baronet.

"From what your groom has told me, your ancestors served their king and country well," said Holmes. "And should not be punished for their misfortune."

"But what of me?" asked the baronet. "I am yet to prove myself."

Holmes began to pace around the room in thought. "Perhaps if you were to become a member of parliament, the Queen might grant you a baronetcy," he said, eventually. "I believe that she is in the habit of giving them out to those who have not done quite enough to deserve a peerage."

"A baronetcy received in that way does not seem like the real thing," said the baronet. "I would prefer to keep this one."

"As you like," said Holmes. "In any case, it is not yet proven beyond reasonable doubt that the baronetcy is extinct."

"It is," said the baronet. "The first baronet was captain of a company that marched to Yarmouth around June 6th, 1667 in case there was a Dutch invasion. The company was not disbanded until mid-August of that year.

Had the second baronet been born late or prematurely, it would have been recorded. The case for illegitimacy is now watertight."

"No case is watertight," said Holmes. "Documents may contain information that is in error or incomplete."

"Well, the situation is less than satisfactory."

"That may be," said Holmes. "However, I regret that the matter is out of my hands."

The baronet did not seem annoyed. "You are right," he said, graciously. "I presume you will be returning to London very soon. I shall let you know of the outcome of the situation, should you still be remotely interested."

"I would like to know the outcome," said Holmes. At this, we departed from the manor for the second time.

"I was sorry we could not do more for that poor baronet," I said, as we began the journey back to London. "It was not his fault that he was of illegitimate descent."

"All the evidence indicates that he was so," said Holmes. "However, my instincts point in the opposite direction. There was not the slightest rumour of illegitimacy in the village. That is most peculiar. Had the wife of the first baronet conducted an adulterous affair during his absence, it would not have gone unnoticed, I am sure."

"Maybe they just did not let on to us," I said. "We were 'gentlemen', remember, and not of their class."

"None the less, we would have discovered such a rumour, had there been one," said Holmes. "I am very much afraid that I may have overlooked something, as I occasionally do. But I cannot think what."

Back in Baker Street, everything returned to normal. I completely forgot about the issue of the baronetcy until the spring of the following year, when Holmes received a letter written on paper of the most expensive kind.

"It is from the baronet," said Holmes. "He is now involved in a court case to settle the question as to whether the Rakestraw Baronetcy is extinct or extant. The case is ongoing here in London. As yet, it has escaped the attention of the newspapers. However, it may become publicized at some point during the trial."

"If it does, the fashionable novelists will make the most of it," I said. "By writing embellished versions."

"As you do with my cases," said Holmes. He continued to read the letter. "The baronet is wary of his chances. However, he understands that there is nothing that I can do."

"In other words, do something right away," I said.

Holmes looked up from the letter. "I have had a thought," he said. "It might be worth our sitting in on the proceedings. If you will accompany me to the court, we can take our place in the gallery."

"What, now?" I asked.

"Yes. Time is of the essence," said Holmes.

I could not think what Holmes hoped to achieve by this; however, within five minutes we were in a cab heading for Fleet Street. As always, the city was a motley crowd of pedestrians and vehicles of every kind.

"The court has been adjourned," the clerk in the entrance hall informed us. "The proceedings will be resumed at two o'clock this afternoon."

"Now what are we going to do?" I asked of Holmes, when we were outside again.

"We shall head for the tavern across the street," said

Holmes, heading straight into the manic traffic. "That is where they will be lunching."

It was as crowded inside the tavern as out. However, I succeeded in spotting the baronet, in a corner at the back of the room. We went over to where he was sitting. He stood up at once, an expression of delight upon his features.

"Mr. Holmes!" he exclaimed. "I was not expecting to see you again."

"I have had an idea since we last met," said Holmes. "It may come to nothing, but I am sure that you would wish to leave no stone unturned."

"Anything, Mr. Holmes," said the baronet.

"I would like to re-examine the register of baptisms for the year 1668," said Holmes. "Would it be possible for me to do so today?"

"In the presence of my solicitor, I should think so," said the baronet.

"Then let us do so at the first possible opportunity," said Holmes. "Preferably before two o'clock, when the case is due to resume."

"Both barristers are at lunch now," said the baronet. "In their chambers. However, I will arrange for a short meeting just before the session is due to resume." The crowd in the tavern was beginning to subside slightly. At a quarter to two, we headed back into the court building.

"Mr. Holmes is a consulting detective and friend of mine," said the baronet, when the barrister finally re-emerged from his private apartment. "He would very much like to check one or two details concerning the evidence. Could he see the parish record of baptisms for the year 1668?"

"I don't see why not," said the barrister. "I am free to examine the evidence at any time. The volume is currently in the courtroom. I shall go and get it." The barrister walked off, his cape flowing behind him, and returned a minute or two later with the book. He then led us into a room nearby, with oak panelling and oak furniture. We sat down at the table provided.

"Now, let us see," said Holmes. He opened the volume and searched carefully for the relevant page. On finding it, he took out a magnifying glass from his pocket and closely examined the record.

"It is as I thought," he said, eventually. "We are saved."

"Are you sure, Holmes?" I asked, trying to contain my excited tone. My friend would undoubtedly explain himself, as he always did.

"Quite sure. My only regret is that I did not observe the date of birth of the second baronet more closely before. It had the appearance of authenticity. And authentic it is, I am sure; at least, for the most part."

"What do you mean, Mr. Holmes?" asked the baronet.

"I have no doubt that the record of birth was written by a cleric of the time," said Holmes. "However, a slight alteration to it could have the most profound of consequences."

"A slight alteration?"

Holmes produced a piece of paper and pencil from his pocket, upon which he scribbled the number 1663.

"It was 1668, not 1663," said the baronet.

"That is easily remedied," said Holmes, drawing on the paper again. He turned it towards the baronet. The number now read 1668.

"It is with the greatest of ease that a 3 can be turned

into an 8," said Holmes. "That was all Miss Rakestraw needed to do. The record of the birth of the second baronet originally read '2nd April 1663', not '2nd April 1668'. Miss Rakestraw changed it. The baptism was on 28th April, 1668 so as a result the interval of twenty-six days between the birth and baptism would look very natural. However, in reality, the baptism took place five years after the birth."

"May I take a look through your glass?" asked the barrister.

"By all means," said Holmes, handing it to him. No longer did my friend appear dejected. He sat confidently beside the barrister as the latter perused the evidence through the glass.

"Good Heavens," exclaimed the lawyer. "Under scrutiny, there is no doubt that such an alteration has been made, albeit carefully done. It was not observed before, because no one was looking for it. This puts a very different light on the matter. I believe it is now an open and shut case."

"Oh, I am so relieved," said the baronet. "You cannot think what this means to me."

"The case will be thrown out as soon as this evidence is presented," went on the barrister. "I am most impressed, Mr. Holmes. If you don't mind me asking, what made you think of this?"

"The baronet's letter to me," said Holmes. "It was handwritten, and dated April '83. It was then that it occurred to me how similar a 3 and an 8 are, and how easy it would be to turn the one into the other. No other alteration to the date could have been made without the alteration being obvious. It would also explain why the birth was recorded along with the baptism, for this was often done when the two events occurred years apart from each other. I really should have thought of this at the time."

"Do not chastise yourself, Mr. Holmes," said the baronet. "No one has a brain that works as fast as that. You have saved not only my identity but also my prosperity; I am forever in your debt."

This last phrase was one that was often uttered by Holmes' clients and there was no doubt in my mind that the baronet would honour such a debt. With so many grateful clients, I wondered just how deep Holmes' purse was these days.

A clerk opened the door. "The court is about to resume, Mr. Copper," he said.

"We shall be there directly," said the barrister. "I shall present this new evidence to the judge at once. Would you care to sit in on the proceedings, Mr. Holmes?"

"I should prefer not to stare down at them from the gallery like a vulture," said Holmes. "However, I believe that there is another case of interest going on in another courtroom. The evidence for the case of The Crown versus Higgins from fifty years ago is to be re-examined. His relatives believe him to have been innocent. I, personally, think that he was guilty. I should like to know what has been discovered."

"As you wish," said the barrister. He and the baronet left the chamber and disappeared back into the courtroom again.

The case that Holmes had chosen to observe was remarkably dry in its procedure, despite its original sensationalism. For half-an-hour he sat at the front of the gallery, with an immobile posture and unconvinced expression. Down below at the front of the court sat what must have been the relatives of the allegedly wronged culprit. From the way that things were progressing, it would appear that the original verdict was in no way challenged. However, as point after point was dragged before the court, there was no end in sight to the tedium. I was relieved when the baronet appeared at the gallery door. We followed him out and back into the hallway downstairs. Before the baronet had a chance to inform us of the developments, a woman with golden curls and flashing eyes suddenly appeared before us. Her being conveyed the presence of great physical energy. She turned her attention to the baronet.

"You think yourself so clever and righteous," she said. "But you are nothing but a fop. Have you any idea what it is like to have to live on your wits day after day with no respite? Why should I live in poverty whilst you live in luxury? I am as much of a baronet in blood as you. If you will not help your poor relations you can expect them to help themselves."

"I would not press this matter," said the baronet, in a low, cautious tone. "As a result of your underhand actions, you are in danger of charges being brought against you. Have a care." With this, the eighth Baronet Rakestraw turned and walked slowly away from the irate woman, towards the exit of the building. We followed him discreetly.

"I suggest that we take tea at the Café Royale," he said when we were all outside, his tone changed to one of carefree gaiety. "And dine at Romano's. What do you say, Mr. Holmes? It will be at my expense, of course."

"An excellent idea," said Holmes. "What do you say, Watson?"

"I should be delighted," I said.

The Chesham Hall Mystery

Although I have included many of Holmes' adventures in my reports, the collection is by no means exhaustive. While sorting through some papers that I had not looked at for some time, I came across a case that had escaped publication but was nevertheless worthy of it. I immediately endeavoured to rectify this situation by writing down its particulars without delay.

During the first few days of April 1896, the sky was continually overcast without ever breaking into rain. The mood of the weather was matched only by that of Holmes; with no case to intrigue him, he had fallen into a depression that had lasted longer than usual. For three days he had received no letters at all, let alone one of interest. It was on such days that I fervently wished for a client to be seen advancing along Baker Street, bringing a matter of so unusual a nature that it would lift Holmes out of his stupor in an instant. While I sat at breakfast he refused to eat, but instead lounged in his armchair by the fire with a cup of coffee, airing his views and grievances.

"It is not the danger or colourfulness of my client's predicament that concerns me," he was saying, determined that I should understand his interest. "It is purely the logic of the case that is of any importance. The whereabouts of a missing object could have more logical scope than the most sensational murder since Jack the Ripper."

"That was one series of murders that you never solved," I said, hoping to challenge him out of his torpid mood.

"There was no data," cried Holmes, exasperatedly. "The evidence was always unwittingly destroyed by the police, whether it was the Metropolitan or the City police. Never before have I come across such a bunch of bungling idiots. Instead of working together, the two forces were working against each other. As a result, the whole case was full of red herrings."

"Well, it would appear that the murderer is no longer at large," I said. "For the murders stopped as mysteriously as they started."

"If I had had full rein of the case, the murderer would have got no further than one murder, and the lives of four other girls would have been saved."

"Ha! So you see, then. It is not just the logic of the case that interests you. It is the usefulness that you can provide."

"Merely a side-effect of my logical work."

"I don't believe you. In any case, I thought that there were seven murders in total."

"Five. The first two were completely unconnected with the others. That much I was able to deduce."

I was about to ask Holmes how he had come to this conclusion, when I heard the clanging of the bell downstairs. Glancing quickly out of the bow window I immediately discerned that my wish had been granted in that a client had materialized in the form of a woman.

She was shown into the large, airy sitting room which

doubled as Holmes' consulting room. I immediately realized that the lady who stood before us was of an affluent disposition, for she wore the latest in high fashion and had the stance of one who has recently come into wealth. Other than this, I could deduce little else, and would have to rely on Holmes or the lady herself to provide further information. Holmes did not appear to be as interested as I had hoped he would be.

"Do sit down," he said, in his customary affable manner, which always seemed to put the client at ease, at least to the extent that was possible, considering their circumstances. He then stretched out his thin legs before the fire, and bade the lady to begin.

"I must stress that my business cannot be considered to be of an urgent nature," said the lady, placing her umbrella aside. "If you have clients with a more pressing need for your invaluable assistance, I am quite prepared to wait."

"You are fortunate," said Holmes. "Never have times been so slack for me. Pray tell me exactly what it is that is perplexing you."

"It is a little mystery concerning a member of my family," began the lady. "My name is Lady Waterston. Three months ago I inherited the ancestral home. Not that it was of the palatial variety; it was really quite modest as ancestral homes go but it did have the title of 'Hall'. Chesham Hall is its name; it is situated about a mile and a half from the town of Chesham, in Buckinghamshire."

"How very fortunate for you," said Holmes.

"Yes," said Lady Waterston. "So much so that I have no problems at all with which to occupy myself. I am therefore obliged to solve problems of a more academic nature, such as the one that I wish to present you with."

Holmes looked a little more like his own self now, keen and alert.

"Please continue," he said.

"The mystery concerns the strange disappearance of my great-aunt. Her name was Cressida Waterston and she lived in Chesham Hall with her parents Lord and Lady Waterston, a sister and two brothers. About fifty years ago, that is to say, in June 1846, my great-aunt was betrothed to a man whom she did not love. The marriage had been arranged by her father, who would not take no for an answer. He threatened her with the prospect of destitution, should she refuse to comply with his wishes. The night before the wedding, she was locked in her bed-chamber, so that she might not abscond from the house in a last fit of desperation. When morning came, her father unlocked the door to her room, and to his amazement, she was not there. Of course, he looked in the wardrobe and behind the curtain and all sorts of odd places like that, but she was nowhere to be found. The window was slightly open, as might be expected on a warm June night, but as the room was situated on the second floor such a mode of escape would have been rather difficult."

"Are you sure she was ever in the room in the first place?" asked Holmes, as Lady Waterston paused in her account.

"It was reported that she was. Though nothing can be certain in this case other than the fact that my great-aunt disappeared. It was fifty years ago."

"Quite," said Holmes. "One must always be careful to distinguish between accurate and inaccurate data. Only accurate data should be used in the process of deductive reasoning. Do go on."

"When it became clear that my great-aunt was not in the room, a thorough search of the house and grounds was made. This proved to be entirely fruitless. One theory that prevailed at the time was that she might have got trapped somewhere in the house; but in fifty years she is still yet to be found."

"Most intriguing," said Holmes. "This case may prove to provide some interest beyond the superficial after all."

I glanced gratifyingly at Holmes, relieved that he would have no use for his usual methods to combat his darkest of moods. A thought struck me, which I felt apt to voice.

"Were all her clothes still in the room after she disappeared?" I enquired.

"Her cloak was not there," answered Lady Waterston, immediately. "As far as all that is known, none of her other clothes were missing."

"Well then, surely it is obvious that she must have left the house," said I, wondering why Lady Waterston had not mentioned this earlier in her account.

"Wait," said Holmes. "That is an assumption. The first task in solving a case is to strip it of all assumptions that may have inadvertently been made. Lady Waterston, has the bedchamber from which your great-aunt disappeared been touched since the morning of her wedding?"

"Yes, it has," said Lady Waterston. "It has been spring-cleaned and the linen changed many times."

"That is indeed a pity," said Holmes. "Though it is as might be expected. I assume that that is the case with the rest of the house?"

"Well, there is one room in the house which has not been touched for well-nigh forty years. Ten years after this unfortunate episode, my great-aunt's father died abruptly. His second wife, that is to say, my great-aunt's stepmother, was so sentimental in her feelings towards her husband that she forbade any of the servants to enter the room; it was to be left exactly as it was on the day he last occupied it. She is no longer living; however the study has remained undisturbed."

"That could be of great use," said Holmes. "Tell me, how old was your great-aunt when she disappeared?"

"Twenty. She would now be ..."

"Seventy. Have you any idea where your great-aunt might have gone, had she left the house?"

"There was nowhere for her to go. She had no close relatives or friends outside the house. All her life she had been what is known as the 'Indoor Type'. Had she gone out into the world alone she would have had nothing but the workhouses and the asylums for the houseless poor to protect her."

"No doubt such places keep registers of the inmates and possibly for a considerable period of time," said Holmes. "But even if such registers still exist, had she called upon these places, she might well have used a false name. Do you have a picture of the missing lady?"

"There is but one picture of her," said Lady Waterston. "A portrait, that hangs on the first floor landing of Chesham Hall. It was painted when she was nineteen years old, not long before her disappearance."

"In that case we may have a means to identify her, should she have fallen into the hands of the Government.

However, before pursuing that line of enquiry I would very much like to see the house."

"The house is at your disposal," said Lady Waterston.

"Excellent. In that case, would it be convenient for us to visit it this afternoon?"

"That would be more than convenient," said Lady Waterston. "I have a shopping expedition to undertake, however I should easily be back by three this afternoon."

"In that case we shall be there at three," said Holmes, getting to his feet. "If you will just give me the precise address." Lady Waterston produced her card.

"I am relieved that you do not find my case too trivial or unimportant," she said, handing it to him.

"Not at all," said Holmes. "I am inclined to think that it is neither."

Lady Waterston duly left our rooms, walking off down the street with her umbrella in a leisurely fashion.

"Well, what do you make of it, Holmes?" I asked, unable to make much of it myself.

"A diversion at worst. Profound at best."

"Have you formed any theories?"

"Not yet. It is a capital mistake to theorize before all the data has been collected. As yet, I have no data. It is all anecdotal and hearsay. I hope to discover evidence on a more solid level when we reach the house."

"We?"

"Yes. I would like you to accompany me as I do on most occasions of this nature. That is, if you have nothing better to do."

"As it is, I have not," said I. "My diary has of late been almost as empty as yours. My patients seem to be unusually healthy this spring."

"Well, then we shall take the Metropolitan Railway from Baker Street to Chesham, where we shall hire a trap to take us the extra mile and a half to Chesham Hall".

"Do you think that we shall be staying the night in the locality?"

"Very possibly. A few essentials might not come amiss."

The journey out from London was surprisingly short in terms of time. Holmes' client had certainly made that part of the exercise most easy to perform. The house at which we soon arrived was still in a state of relative isolation, despite the rows upon rows of newly-built terraced houses that appeared to be advancing towards the locality at an alarming rate. It was as Lady Waterston had said: large for a house but small for a manor. Two rows of windows looked out from the lichen-blotched walls, with a third floor with smaller windows below a slanted roof. A private driveway led up to the entrance, along which we proceeded until the trap came to a stop outside the imposing front doors. A servant came out onto the porch to greet us: she was a woman of sixty, all though possibly more, for she may have looked young for her years. She was unusually cool for a servant but had the air of professionalism associated with a housekeeper.

Holmes jumped down from the trap, followed by our client and myself. We were led into the central hallway of the house, with its customary trophies and carved oak chairs. Lady Waterston asked us if we would like to take tea in the drawing-room but Holmes seemed eager to start work at once and asked to be shown the room from which the great-aunt had so mysteriously disappeared.

"I will show you," said Lady Waterston, and began

to walk up the shallow, carpeted staircase that led away from the central hall area. "It is on the second floor, facing the garden." On the landing, she paused in front of a large painting of a young girl with chestnut hair that hung from behind her head in waves.

"This is my great-aunt, Cressida Waterston," she said.

I was expecting Holmes to admire it for its artistry, for artistic it was; but instead, he commented on the use of linseed and walnut oil. He then added that a palette knife had been used to apply some of the paint.

"Let us now see the bedroom from which she disappeared," he said, finally, upon which we ascended to the second floor.

The bedroom struck me as singularly uninteresting. On one side was a window, out of which the great-aunt might have flown. Holmes immediately went over to it and with Lady Waterston's permission, unfastened the clasp. He then leant out.

"There is nothing fixed to the wall that she could have clambered down," he said, pulling his head back into the room again. "And if she had used a climbing device of her own, no doubt it would have been left hanging for all to see. She would have needed an accomplice to escape in this manner; or indeed, if she escaped through the doorway. Did she have a lover of her own choosing at the time of her wedding?"

"I do not believe so," said Lady Waterston. "Though anything is possible. It is recorded that she did not often go out, and few visitors came to the house".

"One of the servants, maybe?"

"I do not know," said Lady Waterston.

"We shall have to leave open the possibility that an

accomplice helped her to escape. He or she might have had access to the key."

"But you do not favour that possibility?"

"As yet, I do not favour any of the possibilities. There are two cases that we must consider: one: she was locked in this chamber the night before her wedding, as claimed. Two: she was never in the room to start with. We shall consider these two cases separately. In the first case, there are three further possibilities: one: that she found a mode of escape from the bedchamber, either through the window or the doorway. Two: that she was hiding in the room when the search was made and was not found; this is unlikely, for there are not many places to hide in this room. Three: that there is a secret passage or room that leads off this room, in which she hid, until the door to the bedchamber was finally unlocked."

"Secret passage?"

"Indeed. I have made a small study of the subject and have found that the most popular location for a secret passage is behind wainscoting. However, of that, there is none in this room. The second most popular place for a secret room or passage is behind a fireplace. In the case of a secret room it will most probably have the benefit of a fireplace itself, with a flue that connects to the main chimney."

The large, ornate fireplace on one side of the room had now become the focus of attention. Above it was a marble mantelpiece and above this, a gilt framed mirror. It appeared not to have been in recent use although a poker and shovel stood at one side. Holmes and I went over to it. On preliminary examination, nothing appeared out of place; as Holmes stuck his head up the chimney flue a large clod of soot fell down, indicating that the chimney had not been cleaned for months.

"There should be a lever here somewhere," he said, his voice muffled in the chimney. "Ah! I have found it." A moment later the back of the fireplace slid across to reveal a gaping hole. Without hesitation, he advanced into the darkness, whereupon I followed him. We found ourselves standing in a room measuring about eight foot by ten; in the dim light I could make out a table and chair. A lady's outdoor cloak was thrown carelessly over the chair and on the table stood an empty, old-fashioned glass bottle and an empty glass, together with a candle that had burnt all the way down to the holder, covering it in wax.

"Well," said I. "It is as if she had only just left the room."

"Indeed," said Holmes. "And I believe we have now found the missing cloak." He lifted it from the chair; it was remarkably dust-free, considering how long it must have lain there. He emerged from the fireplace into the bedchamber again, carrying the cloak.

"What do you have there?" exclaimed Lady Waterston.

"It is a lady's cloak that may have belonged to your great-aunt. Do you recognize it?"

"No, but it is in the fashion of the 1840s, of which I am familiar," said Lady Waterston.

"Well then, it would seem very possible that your great-aunt hid in the secret room on the morning of the wedding, and remained there while the search for her was on. The back of the fireplace has a closing mechanism on both sides. Some hours later, when she believed all to be quiet in the house, she re-emerged, and left the bed chamber by the door which was by that time unlocked."

"Well, that solves the most perplexing part of the mystery," said Lady Waterston. "I am most grateful, Mr. Holmes. However, I am still very interested to know what happened to her after that."

Holmes laid the cloak upon the cushioned seat at the dressing-table. "The fact that she did not take her cloak with her on leaving the secret room suggests one thing; that she was not intending to leave the house for any length of time."

"Good Heavens, Holmes," I exclaimed. "Do you mean to say that we are going to find her somewhere in the house?"

"I do not have all the data I need," said Holmes, disappearing back through the hole again. This time I did not follow him. When conducting his inspections he was always in another world, focussing entirely upon his observations. A few minutes later, he reappeared with a smile which I found most encouraging.

"I have found a hair," he said. "A long strand of human hair, chestnut in colour. It appears to be very similar to the hair possessed by your great-aunt, as depicted by the painter of her portrait."

"Yes," responded Lady Waterston. "It is identical."

"Do you have an envelope?" asked Holmes.

Lady Waterston took one of the personalized stationery envelopes from the writing table in one corner of the room and handed it to Holmes, whereupon he carefully placed the hair within it.

"Come," he said. "There is more work to be done. Would you be so good as to show me to the study that you believe to have been undisturbed for forty years? That is, if I may be allowed to disturb it."

"Well, my aunt would most probably not have allowed it," said Lady Waterston. "But I am the Lady of the Manor, now. You have my permission to do as you feel fit."

The study was on the ground floor of the house. It was as Lady Waterston had said and had accumulated much dust over the years. Everything that you might expect to find in such a room was there; a large, mahogany desk with green, baize lining and a silver inkwell stand upon it took pride of place; the well stained with ink. The room was further furnished with a few elegant armchairs, a little table and a tall bookcase. Holmes immediately set to work, systematically examining everything with his magnifying glass. Finally, he stood up, having apparently found nothing.

"Lady Waterston, do you have anything that I can stand on?" asked Holmes.

"There should be a step-ladder in the cupboard in the hallway," she replied. I went to get it. It was only two steps high. Holmes placed them in front of the bookcase and went up. The top of the bookcase appeared to be very dusty, even more so than the rest of the room, throwing up clouds of white particles at the slightest disturbance.

"This is all the proof I need," said Holmes, returning to ground level. He held out a strand of hair that looked similar to the other.

"If these two samples of hair match, we have but one possibility," said Holmes.

"What," said I, in my usual state of confusion at this stage in a case.

"That great-aunt Cressida never left the house."

"Never left the house? You mean, she is still in the house?"

"Exactly; and I have a theory as to as to where in the house we shall find her."

"Where?" I asked, incredulously.

"Consider the facts. A hair almost certainly belonging to Cressida was found in the secret chamber, as was her cloak, which she did not take with her when she left the room. Another sample of hair, probably belonging to Cressida, is also found in the study, on top of the book-case. Do you not see the obvious conclusion?"

"Well, I don't see how it could have floated up onto the top of the bookcase. Unless she herself were standing on the steps."

"Exactly," said Holmes. "She was, most probably, standing on some steps. Why would she be doing that?"

"To access the books on the top shelves, I suppose," I said.

"There are no books on the top shelves."

"Well, there might have been before the room was left in the state that it is now."

"You can think of no other explanation."

"As to why she should be teetering on the top of a step-ladder? No, I am afraid I cannot; unless it was to perform some task such as cleaning, dusting or painting. But I cannot imagine why a lady of her standing would be doing any of those tasks."

"I believe there is one person who might be able to enlighten you," said Holmes, still determined to tantalize me. "Lady Waterston, would you be so good as to call the housekeeper?"

"Why yes," said she, and immediately glided over to the bell-pull and tugged at it. Despite its lack of use for forty years, it still appeared to function, for within minutes, the housekeeper appeared, with the same composure with which I had first seen her.

"Please sit down," said Holmes. The housekeeper appeared uncomfortable.

"It is not my place to be seated upstairs in my employer's house," she said, and remained standing.

"Is it not? I find that surprising," said Holmes. "I would have thought that you were very used to sitting in this house."

The housekeeper's composure finally seemed to have been rattled. "I do not know what you mean, sir," she said, looking as though she would like to leave the room.

"Do you not," said Holmes. "Well, then you shall be interviewed standing. In which year did you commence working here?"

"It was in 1846, sir. I started out as scullery maid."

"Which month in 1846? Can you remember?"

"It would have been June, sir."

"June: The month of Miss Cressida's wedding."

"Yes, that is correct, sir."

"Did you know Cressida Waterston?"

"No, sir. A scullery maid rarely, if ever, sees anything that goes on upstairs. But I knew of her and her disappearance on the day of her wedding."

"Which was shortly before your own appearance here."

"Yes, sir. It was the day after the wedding that I started here."

"The wedding that never took place."

"Yes, sir."

I began to see dimly what Holmes was driving at.

"How long were you a scullery maid?" went on Holmes.

"Not five years, sir. I was then promoted to housemaid, upon which I had a welcome change of duties."

"Indeed. And I presume that one of your duties was to dust the upstairs rooms in the house, including the ground floor."

"Yes, sir."

"Including this study, in fact."

"I have not dusted this study for forty years," said the housekeeper. "But yes, I would have dusted it on a very regular basis."

"Was Lord Waterston ever in the study while you were dusting it?"

"No, sir. He had given strict instructions that whenever he was in his study he was not to be disturbed."

"So you did not see much of Lord Waterston."

"No, sir. There was one occasion, however, when I was handing around the sandwiches in the drawing-room. He looked directly at me in the strangest of manners. At that moment, I thought that he had recognized me. But then he looked away again."

"Recognized you?"

"Well, yes. It is true that I was wearing my cap and apron, and that my hair was cropped, but you would have thought he would still recognize his own child."

"You are Cressida," I gasped.

"Yes," said Cressida. "Although for the last fifty years I have been known as Cassie, and then as Mrs. Bridcastle."

"Now will you sit down," said Holmes, offering her one of the George III armchairs.

"Yes, I believe I will," said Cressida. She sat down, with the full arrogance and bearing of an aristocrat; the humble, degrading housekeeper's uniform that she wore did not detract from her obvious high birth. Without prompting, she began to speak further on the matter concerned.

"On the night before my wedding, I was in a state of absolute desperation. I could not sleep at all. By dawn, I had become so desperate that I embarked upon a plan. For twenty-four hours while they searched for me I hid in the secret chamber that lies behind the fireplace of my bedroom. My father was unaware of its existence. Early in the morning of the following day, I emerged from the chamber and found that the door was now unlocked. I changed into modest clothing and cut my hair. I then wrote myself a reference and left the house by the front door, returning to it at the back, where I presented myself at the servants' entrance in the guise of an applicant for the position of scullery maid. This position I got. None of the servants appeared to recognize me, or if they did, they said nothing."

"And you have remained here ever since."

"Yes. Eventually I was promoted to the position of housekeeper, which is how you find me today."

"Well, you certainly cannot continue to work in such a position," said Lady Waterston. "I never really considered you as a servant, anyway. From now on, you shall live as you should have done in the last fifty years. Mr. Holmes," she said, turning to my friend with a satisfied expression. "If you will wait a moment, I shall present you with a cheque. You have demonstrated what a simple matter it is to solve a case, when one goes about it in the right way. It appears to me to be so easy that I have a mind to become a detective myself."

"I feel that I shall have to become more reticent in

my explanations," said Holmes, "Or I shall lose my reputation. By all means, set yourself up as a detective. There are already hundreds in London, some of whom are women."

"Here is the cheque, Mr. Holmes," said Lady Waterston. Holmes took it without even looking at it. As we left the house, Holmes informed me that his ancestors had been country squires, a fact that he had told me before, but seemed to want to emphasise at that moment. It was not like him to worry about his place in society. I assured him that aristocratic or not, he was and always would be the greatest detective of them all.

The Unique Case

Some years ago, Holmes was engaged in a most singular case. His client at the time asked me specifically not to reveal her real name or the location of her ancestral home, should I ever come to chronicling the adventure. Respecting her wishes I shall refer to her throughout this account as Lady Rossetti and shall say only that the events took place in England.

It was in the autumn of 1894 that Lady Rossetti made the acquaintance of Sherlock Holmes. She appeared late one afternoon and was shown in, as clients who appeared on the doorstep always were, without an appointment. She could have been no more than nineteen. Some would have been shocked by the manner in which she presented herself; long, wavy hair that was obviously dyed hung outrageously about a voluptuous body wrapped in the folds of a dress that was well ahead of the current fashion. She sat opposite Holmes in tense anticipation, gazing up at him with wild eyes and pouting lips. Her nervous state aroused my curiosity as to what was troubling her. When Holmes enquired as to this, she said:

"Nothing is troubling me, Mr. Holmes. I merely wish to locate the family jewels."

"You have family jewels?" responded Holmes.

"We had family jewels. They disappeared around about 1650, at the time of the Revolution. My family was Royalist, you see. My ancestor, Sir —, is alleged to have hidden the jewels lest the enemy should find them. They have remained hidden ever since. After the Restoration, an attempt was made to find them but without success."

"Have you yourself attempted to find them?" asked Holmes.

"I would not know where to start," said the lady.

"Who told you that the jewels existed?" asked Holmes.

"My parents."

"Who live at the manor."

"Not really," she replied. "They spend very little time there, for they find it as dull as ditch water and prefer to mix amongst the rich and famous in London. I live more or less alone in the manor, with only the servants for company."

"The manor is located ... where?"

"In — shire," replied the lady. "It is an estate of some three thousand acres, with farmland, woodland, gardens and grounds."

"How long has this estate been in your family?"

"It has always been in my family. The house was built in 1642."

"So your ancestor, Sir —, lived there."

"Oh, yes. It was he who built the house."

"Then it might be helpful if we were to visit the house and land."

"You would be most welcome to, Mr. Holmes," said she, enthusiastically. "There are many guest rooms available."

"Excellent," said Holmes. "Then Dr. Watson and I shall travel down there at our earliest convenience."

"Dr. Watson?"

"Yes. I would like him to accompany me to assist in the investigation."

A frown traversed the lady's pre-Raphaelite features.

"Does he really have to come?"

"You would prefer it if Dr. Watson did not come?"

"Well, yes. But if he must ..."

"Why is it that you do not wish Dr. Watson to come?"

"I have nothing against Dr. Watson," said the lady. "It is just that ..."

"Just what?"

"I would rather that you came alone."

"But why?"

"Never mind," said the lady. "If you wish for Dr. Watson to come, then come he shall. There is an end to the matter. "Now," she said, producing a velvet pouch. "Here is the money for the train tickets. You will be met at the railway station by my groom, who will transport you by coach to the manor. It is three miles from the station."

"Capital," said Holmes. "You may expect us in the next few days, tomorrow even, maybe. We will send you a telegram in advance of our arrival."

"That's splendid," said the lady. She appeared over-joyed at the prospect of Holmes' arrival. She stood up and hurried out of the room, as if she were afraid that he might change his mind.

"Well," I said when she was out of the door. "What do you think of that?"

"There is something not quite right in this case," said

Holmes, taking up a glowing cinder with the tongs and lighting his pipe. "I felt it from the start."

"I thought that you never felt your way towards your conclusions," I said. "Feelings are not rational."

"That is not entirely true," said Holmes. "An instinctive feeling can have arisen from subconscious realizations. The mind observes, deduces and concludes, without the knowledge of the thinker. But when the evidence that these deductions are based on comes from a woman ...you are right, Watson, I should disregard these feelings. It is impossible to build upon the behaviour of a woman."

"You found her behaviour suspect?"

"Yes," replied Holmes. "All throughout the interview she appeared shifty and furtive. No doubt, however, all will eventually become clear."

It happened that Holmes' affairs were in a sufficient state of order that we were able to set out the following day. As usual, we travelled by train; we seemed to be spending our life on trains these days, for Holmes' activities were taking him all over the country. I did not mind, for I was having quite a time gallivanting around as Holmes' assistant. On this occasion we were seated in one of the first class compartments for the money which Lady Rossetti had given us for the fare was more than enough. It was all very agreeable.

Hours later, the train chugged into our station. A groom was there waiting to meet us, as promised. We were then treated to a scenic tour of the open countryside, with its green pastures, meadows and stone bridges thrown over burbling streams and gushing rivers. The manor was an old, rambling house with weatherworn walls, pointed gables and windows with narrow panes set together. The lawns surrounding it were immaculately mown and the hedges beside it cut in elegant topiary. Lady Rossetti herself came out of the stone archway entrance onto a gravelled circular area to greet us; she wore an odd sort of robe that looked more like a cloak, and was followed by a smartly dressed footman, who began unloading our two bags. "I am so glad you are here so soon," said Lady Rossetti, looking even more overjoyed than she had at our last meeting. "Please come in." The door through which we came formed part of a much larger arch, bordering an alcove with gigantic stained glass window insets. A long wooden banqueting table that could have been seventeenth century was set against one wall. Upon another wall above a fireplace was a life size portrait of someone who looked rather like Charles I but wasn't. Another footman who matched the first appeared and took our hats and coats.

The luggage now stood in the centre of the hall. "As for the sleeping arrangements," began Lady Rossetti, "There are a number of options. There is the red room, with its own bathroom, where the Queen herself once slept. On the first floor there are four guest bedrooms. Lastly, there is the dressing room alongside my own bedroom. I have had a bed placed in there."

"One of the guest bedrooms on the second floor will suit me admirably," said Holmes.

"Then I shall give you the one with the view," said Lady Rossetti at once. "There is a magnificent view of the whole county from the bedroom on the east side. As for you, Dr. Watson, I shall place you in the room opposite."

"Thank you kindly," I said, wondering if I too, would get a view. It seemed unlikely. The footman picked up our bags and carried them out of the hall. I was hoping that we would now be offered some refreshment, for we had declined to partake of railway fare. However, Holmes had other ideas.

"Perhaps we should start the investigation immediately, while we still have the daylight," he said. "Would it be possible for you to compile a list of everything in the house that is connected with your ancestor, Sir —?. His papers, possessions, private rooms, portraits ..."

"We certainly have a portrait of him," said Lady Rossetti. "As for papers, I would have to look through every paper that is stored in the attic. It could take some time."

"Well, let us see the portrait," said Holmes.

"Certainly," said Lady Rossetti. "It is right here in this hall." And she went over to the Charles I style painting. "This is he," she said, standing beside it in a posture as regal as the subject of the painting himself. "My great - five greats, I believe, grandfather." The portrait appeared to have been painted exactly where it hung, for within it was depicted the very fireplace that stood below it in real form, with the same stone surround and the same brickwork immediately beyond it. Holmes walked up to the painting and stood in front of it.

"That is odd," he said, examining it with his magnifying glass. "Some of the paint is still wet."

"Is it?" said Lady Rossetti. "Well, it has been restored recently."

"That would explain it," said Holmes. "Judging from the background, I assume that it was originally done in this very hall."

"It was," said Lady Rossetti. "Or at least, I presume that it was. The fireplace and its surround are identical."

"As are the bricks," said Holmes. "Although one brick in the painting stands out. It is painted in a detectably darker hue than are the others. This is not the case with the real fireplace."

I looked down at the fireplace. It was true. All the bricks were the same colour, but on the painting, one stood out. "I do not believe it to be accidental," said Holmes, now examining the bricks in question with his magnifying glass. "I believe that this is the brick that is indicated on the painting. It is loose."

"Oh, this is exciting," said Lady Rossetti, jumping up and down.

"Yes," said Holmes, somewhat dryly. With a bit of manipulation, the brick slid out in his hand. A dark space was now visible in the place where the brick had been and beyond.

"Well, I never," I said. Holmes examined the hollow area and brought out an old, folded parchment.

"This case seems to be progressing remarkably quickly," said Holmes. "Let us see what is on this parchment. May I use this table?"

"Yes," said Lady Rossetti. Holmes carefully unfolded the stiff parchment paper and spread it out upon the table. It was about a foot square, browned and mottled, with wear bordering on breakage along the creases. Upon it, in ink, was drawn a map, apparently of an island, with a circular construction in the middle. This place was marked with a cross. In the corner, in copper plate writing, were inscribed the compass points North, South, East and West.

"This is like Treasure Island," I exclaimed. "It's a treasure map."

"Indeed," said Holmes. "The position of the 'treasure' is here," he said, indicating the cross.

"The map does not indicate where in the world the island is located," I said. "However, it does have a unique shape. Lady Rossetti, did your ancestor ever travel overseas?"

"Yes," said she, with conviction. "He sailed to the Americas on several occasions. There are records and log books of his expeditions somewhere in the house."

"We shall have to look through them carefully," I said. "There is no doubt a record of his visit to this very island. It looks as though we ourselves shall soon be going on a trip. What do you think, Holmes?"

Holmes was examining the parchment paper with his magnifying glass that now appeared to be in constant use. "The parchment has been folded both ways," he said. "Thus increasing the level of wear along the creases."

"Well, that does not tell us where the island is," I said.

"I prefer to adopt a wider field of observation," said Holmes. "Seemingly irrelevant detail can often turn out to be of crucial significance."

At this moment, a gong sounded, which to my relief, announced the commencement of dinner. It appeared that the investigation was at a halt, for we all traipsed into the dining room. Inside, a table with a white table cloth was elegantly laid out for us. Again, I could not help feeling that I had it very easy, these days.

Lady Rossetti now seemed uninterested in discussing the case. Instead, as the champagne was poured by one of the footmen, she began to ask Holmes about his background, a subject on which even I, his closest friend, had scanty knowledge.

"Are you of noble birth, Mr. Holmes?" she enquired.

"My ancestors were country squires," replied Holmes. "However, I believe that 'landed gentry' would be the term used to describe them, not nobility. I, however, have had to make my own way in the world, to a large extent."

"And so you have done, very well," said Lady Rossetti. "With your intellect, you would not be out of place within the highest echelon of society."

"I have certainly been of assistance to various members of the European nobility," said Holmes. "However, I am not at liberty to disclose names."

"Why are you not married, Mr. Holmes?"

Holmes removed his napkin from its holder and placed it on his lap. "I find these questions of a rather too personal nature, and irrelevant to my reason for being here," he said.

"Oh, I am sorry," said Lady Rossetti. "I will not ask you any more impertinent questions."

"But if you must know, there was one woman whom I would have married, had I had the opportunity."

"Was she good-looking?" enquired Lady Rossetti.

"Yes, most certainly." said Holmes.

"Intelligent?"

"She was my equal."

"Oh, my goodness," said Lady Rossetti, almost spilling her champagne. "Then she was most certainly intelligent. What about her singing?"

"She was at one time, an opera singer."

Lady Rossetti appeared to become ever more agitated.

"And her dancing?"

"Of that, I am unsure. However, her acting was on a professional level."

"And her personality?"

"Of that, I knew little," said Holmes. "I met her on only two occasions. The most memorable two occasions of my life."

"Then perhaps you would have been sick of her in three weeks," said Lady Rossetti.

"Logically speaking, that is indeed possible," said Holmes. "However, I prefer not to imagine such things. As far as I know, I will never have the pleasure of her company for three whole weeks. I would drop the most sensational of cases for such an opportunity."

I was surprised to hear Holmes talk like this. What exactly were his feelings for Irene Adler? He had mentioned her from time to time since that case involving the King of Bohemia and had made it clear how much he admired her, but now it seemed to be reaching a deeper level. I was impressed. However, Lady Rossetti seemed to feel differently about it.

"Where is this woman now?" she asked.

"Not in the country," said Holmes. "I believe she now resides on the continent with her husband."

"Her husband? You mean, she is married?"

"Most definitely," said Holmes. "I myself was present at the wedding."

Lady Rossetti looked somewhat relieved. One of the footmen brought in a gigantic soup tureen from which he ladled out a shallow bowlful of soup to each of us. It looked as though the dinner was going to last some time. I glanced at Holmes, expecting him to have an air of impatience, but he appeared resigned. It was a good one and a half hours before all the courses were got through.

"Well, shall we take coffee in the drawing-room?" said Lady Rossetti, finally. She stood up and headed across the hallway. Holmes and I followed her into a sumptuous, elegant room and sat down in one the armchairs that generously provided itself. Lady Rossetti turned down the gas so that a mellow light effused all around, glinting off the chandelier.

"Mr. Holmes, would you play for us?" asked Lady Rossetti.

Holmes gave a sort of short laugh. "I am afraid I have not brought my violin down with me," he said.

"Oh, that doesn't matter at all," said Lady Rossetti. "For I have one right here." Out of the blue, she produced a wooden violin case and held it out to Holmes invitingly.

"I'm sorry," said Holmes. "But this is not what I was summoned here to do."

"Well, perhaps I could sing something," said Lady Rossetti. "Although I may not be up to the standard of that woman. Would either of you able to accompany me on the pianoforte?"

"No, this really is too much," said Holmes. "Can we please get on with the case. I feel that I am near to solving it." He took out the map from his pocket and spread it out upon the coffee table. "We need not find ourselves ultimately surprised by the form in which the island will take. It may not necessarily be a real island. It could be a picture of an island, or a model. Alternatively, it could be a code. However, we shall, for the time being, assume the most straightforward possibility, that it is a real island.

Now to determine the location of the island. I see no reason why it must lie in a tropical region overseas; it is as likely to lie in the immediate vicinity. Lady Rossetti, do you have a map of the estate and surrounding country?"

"I believe so," said Lady Rossetti. She wafted over to the cabinet, upon which were stacked many cultured books, and opened a drawer, from which she took out a large map of the estate.

"This map was drawn fifty years ago," she said. "It covers most of the estate and some area outside of it." She brought it over to Holmes, who spread it out before him.

"It appears you have a lake on the estate," said Holmes. "With an island in it."

"Yes," said Lady Rossetti. "But it is a very small one."

"If my reasoning is correct, the island drawn on the parchment is also very small," said Holmes. "The building drawn on the map is, I believe, a dovecote. It is circular in shape as dovecotes usually are. Unless it is very unusual, it will not be more than fifteen feet in diameter. If it is drawn to the same scale as the island, it is a very small island indeed; less than a hundred yards across. Lady Rossetti, have you ever visited this island?"

"I have once or twice," she replied. "It is allowed to grow wild and birds flock to it in their thousands."

"Let us proceed there at once," said Holmes. "With luck, the case can be concluded by tonight and we can catch the last train home."

"Oh, no," said Lady Rossetti.

"What is the matter, Lady Rossetti?" I asked.

"I am most disappointed. I was hoping that Mr. Holmes would be staying for at least a week."

"A week?" Holmes turned abruptly to the woman. "Madam, I cannot spare you a whole week. I must be back in London by Friday at the latest."

"Well, at least that gives us a couple of days together," said Lady Rossetti. "I had no idea that you would solve this mystery so quickly. It has baffled my ancestors for generations."

Holmes did not respond, but instead stood up and walked over to the open French windows.

"Which is the quickest way to the lake?" he asked.

"By the path through the woodland," said Lady Rossetti. Across the fields, an area of trees was visible. "But the light is fading, now. It will be dark by the time we get there. Let us postpone the enterprise until tomorrow morning."

"Perhaps you are right," said Holmes. "I am, as it happens, rather tired. I have not slept a full eight hours for many months. If you do not mind, I shall retire immediately."

"All right, if you must," said Lady Rossetti. Holmes quitted the chamber and I was left standing alone with his client. She seemed somewhat distraught and disappointed.

"You must forgive my friend's abruptness," I said. "I have lived with him on and off for many years and have been frequently subjected to it. However, he is above all, a sincere and well-meaning person."

"He is," agreed Lady Rossetti, fervently. "However, I cannot applaud his taste in women. Did you yourself ever meet the one that he was talking about this evening?"

"I caught a glance of her through an open window," I said. "That is all. I cannot give you much of a description."

"Well, at least it shows that he is not one of those, said Lady Rossetti.

"Certainly not," I replied. "And I myself have been married."

Lady Rossetti gave a wan smile. "Perhaps we should also retire now," she said, lighting a candle. "Mr. Holmes will undoubtedly be up at the crack of dawn. We must be ready for him."

I was not particularly tired, but agreed to this. I had brought an interesting book down with me to read at such a time as this. We went upstairs to the corridor where the guest bedrooms lay where we parted and Lady Rossetti went off to her own bedroom. I headed off to my room at the end of the corridor. On entering it I turned up the gas. I then sat at the writing chair provided and began to read.

It must have been twenty minutes of so, when I thought I heard a knock at the door. I went over to see who it was, but on opening it, found that it was Holmes' door, not my own, from where the sound had come. Lady Rossetti appeared to be standing by it, dressed in a white negligee and carrying a candle. A moment later, she knocked again and finally opened the door. Then she walked in, closing the door behind her.

I closed my own door. If Holmes had an assignation with the young woman, that really was no business of mine. I am a man of many faults, but indiscretion is not one to them. No doubt Holmes would tell me all about it in due course if he felt so inclined. I decided to go to bed. About a minute later, I heard a door close and what could only be Lady Rossetti walking softly along the corridor past my room. It appeared that the meeting had been a short one. As it happens, Holmes described to me some days later the brief interlude that had occurred, which I am now in a position to relate: he was not asleep, but lying in bed when the woman knocked at his door. In his drowsy state, he reached for a match with which to light the lamp, when there had been another knock, followed by the door opening. There stood Lady Rossetti. She had let herself in and stood there before him in her nightgown, holding a candle. Dressed in his pyjamas, Holmes sat up in bed and viewed her in alarm.

"What is it that you want, Lady Rossetti?" he whispered. "To discuss the case," she said, advancing towards the bed. She stood at the end of it, in the shadows, gazing at him in a mesmerized manner.

"This is not the time or the place to do so," said Holmes, getting out of bed and walking over to the door. But Lady Rossetti made no attempt to move. She stood, immobile, holding the candle beside her.

"We can continue this conversation in the morning," said Holmes insistently, but still the lady did not move. Holmes went back to the bed again and sat down.

"Lady Rossetti, I am rather tired and if you wish me to continue to give my full attention to the case, I must sleep now," he said. "I shall be up at six o'clock tomorrow morning; we can discuss anything that is preying on your mind at that time."

Lady Rossetti began to walk reluctantly towards the door. Holmes remained seated on the bed. She turned the handle and backed out, staring at him in the same transfixed manner. The door closed behind her. That is much as how I remember his report of the incident.

It was without difficulty that I fell asleep owing to our

long journey and did not awake until the dawn chorus served as a natural alarm clock. I arose almost immediately in a most refreshed state. I wondered if Holmes was already awake. After dressing, I opened my door and found that Holmes' door was ajar. Further investigation revealed that he was not in his room.

I hurried downstairs and into the dining-room, where it appeared that the servants had barely begun their morning duties. A maid was knelt down by the fireplace, cleaning the grate, surrounded by brushes and polish. It was clear that breakfast would be a while. I went out across the hall and into the drawing-room, where I found Holmes standing on the patio just beyond the open French windows, in the company of Lady Rossetti. He turned as I entered the room. "Oh, there you are, Watson," he said. "We were just waiting for you. We were about to walk over to the lake."

"It was good of you to wait for me," I said. "Are you sure that the two of you would not like to go alone?"

"No," said Holmes. "I would like you to come."

"Well, then, let us not waste any more time," I said. We set off along the avenue that led through the back garden with a well-kept lawn on either side which eventually became a shady path through some woodland. Holmes walked on ahead, with Lady Rossetti hurrying along with him and me walking a few paces behind them. We walked some distance through the wood until the landscape opened up again and there was the lake. It reached from one side of the wood to the other. Within it was a little island, thickly overgrown with trees and vegetation, with birds circling over it. Holmes stopped and brought out the map. "It would appear that we are on the south side of the island," he said, perusing it.

"Is that a boathouse up there?" I asked, indicating a hut, adjacent to a jetty that lay some distance from us around the lake.

"Yes," said Lady Rossetti. "That is the boat that I mentioned earlier to Mr. Holmes." We all began walking towards the hut. When we got there, the door was not locked, and inside, much to our delight, was a rowing boat apparently ready for use.

"Could you help me to push the boat out," asked Holmes. I went round to the other side of the boat and between the two of us we were able to shift it onto the water. Lady Rossetti was standing on the jetty platform. Holmes got in and held out his hand to help Lady Rossetti, who clambered in and I sat down upon the bench in the stern. Holmes removed his coat and took the oars. We then glided towards the island in twenty, long strokes, as performed by Holmes, who as usual, was far stronger than anyone would ever have believed. As we approached, the sound of bird calls became ever louder, and the mysterious world within the overgrown island became more visible. When we reached the bank, I tied the chain around a pole that was conveniently stationed there, and stepped onto the grassy ground. Again, Lady Rossetti was chivalrously helped from the boat by Holmes.

There were no paths on the island, so thickly was it covered in plants. "This jungle is like a forgotten world," I said. What looked like a parakeet was perching in one of the trees above. Perhaps one of Lady Rossetti's ancestors had brought it back from his travels. Holmes, however, did not appear to be particularly interested in the exotic wildlife all around him.

"I believe the dovecote will be in that direction," he said, miraculously producing a compass. "If we can walk as best we can in a north westerly direction, we should, with any luck, come across it."

"I wouldn't be too sure of that, Holmes," I said. "With all this vegetation, we cannot walk in the direction of our choosing."

"That will not be a problem," said Holmes. "Someone has walked this route recently. If you will observe the branches of the trees that have been pushed aside and the flattening of the grass, thus making the traces of a path."

"Good Heavens, Holmes," I said. "Does that mean someone has found the treasure before us?"

"There is an alternative explanation," said Holmes. However, he did not venture to say what it was. I and Lady Rossetti continued to follow him, as he wended his way through past the plants and trees. He appeared to know where he was going. I was glad that we were in England, and not in some remote tropical region where natural dangers would be lurking.

Holmes finally stopped in his tracks. He was standing in front of a stone building, covered in vines and with the sides obscured by a mass of plants and vegetation. It appeared to be circular in form. I looked up to see a pointed, red-tiled roof topped by a cedar lantern emerging from the plants.

"You were right that it was a dovecote," I said. "It has not been used for quite a time, I think."

"The entrance is over here," said Holmes, moving back the branches that were clambering around the construction. A solid oak door that could not have been more than three feet high was set in a square archway, which opened with ease. We managed to access the interior which was rather dim and dank. As we walked around inside, our footsteps echoed upon a stone floor. I could just make out hundreds of little nesting enclaves all around the perimeter of the interior. They all appeared to be empty.

"Now what?" I asked. "Where is the treasure?" I looked upwards to where the light was coming in through the cedar lantern that was partially blocked with leaves.

"I believe the stone slabs on the floor are the only possibility," said Holmes. I looked down to see a paving of rough, stone slabs that were worn away at the edges.

"You mean, it is underneath one of these slabs," I said. Holmes knelt down. "One of these slabs has been moved recently," he said. "Whichever it was, it was then placed on this slab. If you will observe the deposit of earth in a rectangular outline." He attempted to lift the neighbouring slab but it was held fast. However, the one next to it came up easily, to reveal a dark space beneath. Inside was an iron casket with a rounded lid.

"I believe that this is what we are looking for," he said, lifting out the casket and giving it a cursory examination. "It is locked," he concluded. He handed the casket to Lady Rossetti. "It is up to you to do what you like with this," he said.

"Let us take it back to the house," said she. "It will have to be forced open."

Holmes appeared strangely uninterested in the contents of the casket as we ambled back to the boat; in fact, his attitude to the whole case had been one of considerable apathy. Usually, when on a case, he would be alive and intent on discovering the truth. But this time, it seemed as though he was only going through the motions. He rowed us back to the bank, from where we returned to the house. On our arrival, Holmes continued in his laconic fashion. Lady Rossetti took us into the drawing-room and placed the casket upon the table, around which we all sat. The footman entered carrying a tool and handed it to Lady Rossetti.

"Now," she said, in a resolute tone. "Now we shall see." The casket lid sprang open to reveal a pile of flat stones. A silence amongst us ensued.

"It looks as though we have been led on a wild goose chase," I said, at length.

"Indeed," said Holmes.

"What do you suggest, Mr. Holmes?" asked Lady Rossetti.

Holmes turned to his client in a most direct manner. "I suggest you tell me why you planned this little venture," he said. "I have no more time to waste on an artificial escapade."

"What do you mean, Holmes?" I asked.

"Throughout this case, there has been one peculiarity after another. Firstly, the wet paint on the portrait. The explanation that the painting was restored recently is plausible; however, I cannot overlook the other possibility, which is that the portrait, although of a seventeenth century person, was painted recently and that the paint is still drying, as paint can do for up to a year after it is applied to a canvas. Then there is the excessive folding of the parchment. It was first folded in one direction and then in the other, producing a very pronounced crease;

why would this have been done? If the map had been folded simply to decrease its size, this would have been unnecessary and destructive. No, it was done because the person who folded it wished the parchment to appear as though it had been folded for a very long time. Finally, there are the tracks that we found on the island, indicating that someone has been to the dovecote recently."

I found all this hard to take in. "Are you saying that someone painted the painting, or rather had it painted by an artist, drew the map or had it drawn, placed it in the space behind the loose brick, went out to the dovecote and placed the casket containing the stones under a slab?" I asked.

"That is exactly what I am saying, Watson."

"But who would do this? And why? And would not Lady Rossetti have noticed if a new painting had suddenly appeared in the Great Hall?"

"That is a very good question, Watson. She would undoubtedly have noticed. Would you not agree, Lady Rossetti?"

Lady Rossetti said nothing. But when neither of us did either, she finally spoke.

"You tell me, Mr. Holmes," she said. "You are the detective, not me."

"Very well, then," said Holmes. "The only theory that will fit all the facts is that you yourself had the portrait of you ancestor painted, specifically instructing the artist to copy the bricks around the fireplace exactly, and to paint one of them darker than the others, the one that you knew was loose, and that had a secret space behind it. You then procured, probably with some difficulty, some seventeenth century parchment paper, on which you instructed that same artist to draw a map of the island in the lake on the estate, using the most old-fashioned ink that you could lay your hands on. You then folded it up and put it in the secret place behind the brick. You then collected some stones, placed them in a casket and took it over to the dovecote on the island, where you hid it underneath a slab. All this, I am sure of; the only thing that I am unsure of is your motive."

Lady Rossetti sat rigidly without smiling. "You shall be paid," she said, after a pause. "You have solved the case remarkably quickly."

"And now, I believe we should be in very good time for the nine o'clock train," said Holmes. He stood up. "We shall go and pack."

"I shall send up the footman to bring down your bags," said Lady Rossetti. "We can have a coach ready for you in half-an-hour." She stared after Holmes in a depressed manner as he left the drawing-room. I was unsure what to say to her, and eventually made my excuses and went upstairs to pack my belongings. As I did so, I was inclined to think that Holmes was being a little foolish; then I remembered his attitude towards those less mentally agile than himself. It is true that he makes an exception with me, but I have never known him to do so with anyone else.

"She was certainly a most eligible woman," I said, when we were finally left at the station in our own company. "How did she appeal to you, Holmes?"

"I found nothing about her to repel me," said Holmes. "However, I believe that were she of middle-class origin, her eccentricity might have seriously compromised her eligibility."

"You are not without eccentricity yourself," I could not help but comment.

"True, but I live on my wits rather than on eligibility."

"We seem to have an increasingly large clientele from a privileged background," I observed.

"That is indeed so," said Holmes. "We have been reduced to gratifying the whims of the upper-class. It is time to start selecting our cases in a less materialistic manner. In future, I shall accept a case purely on its merits, without consideration of the client's purse."

"Well, this time, you were fortunate on both counts," I observed. "It was a most unique case."

"The motive was certainly curious," said Holmes. "I have in the past been involved in cases arising from the strangest of motives and in the most part, have succeeded in discerning it. But I have to admit that on this occasion, as to motive, I am completely baffled."

The Masked Man

On a September morning in 1887, a man whom I recognized as a previous client was shown into our lodgings. It was unusual for Holmes to see the same client twice, causing me to wonder what further business with Holmes the man could have.

"Well," said Holmes, when we were all seated. "How may I help you?"

"Well, it was just a social call, really," said the man, shuffling his feet awkwardly. "I was in the area, and I thought it might be nice to call upon my old acquaintance, Sherlock Holmes."

"So you have no case to present me with?"

"Not really, no," said the man. "Have I come at a bad time?"

"It is not a case of the time. When a client steps into this room, it becomes a consulting room. I am afraid I am not able to assist you in any way other than a professional one."

"Oh," said the man, looking rather dejected. "Well, I had better be going, then. I really thought we had got along famously the last time we met." He stood up and left the room immediately. We could hear him conversing with Mr. Hudson at the bottom of the stairs, no doubt complaining about his reception. After the front door had opened and closed, I noticed that the gentleman had left his cane behind. I pointed this out to Holmes, picking it up and examining it.

"He must want to return," I said. "That is a common reason why an item is mislaid; it is known by psychologists as a parapraxis."

"It looks as though we shall never see the last of him," said Holmes. "However the cane is interesting. I can immediately deduce that it had a previous owner."

"How on earth do you know that?" I asked, incredulously.

"The initials, 'A.T.', at the top of the cane are not his. I can also deduce that the cane has spent some time lying on a roadside. If you will observe a detectable lightening on one side of the curvature whilst the other remains dark. It has been lying in the sun for a matter of days, if not months. The groove cut into it near the end indicates that it has been run over by a cartwheel. The cart was most likely carrying hay, for the groove has the distinctive imprint of the wheels of a hay cart. Furthermore, the roadside was gravel, for there is scratching upon the part of the cane that was resting on the ground."

"Good Heavens, Holmes," I exclaimed. "What was it doing at the edge of the road? It looks as though it was originally rather an expensive one."

"It was," said Holmes. "And can only have belonged to a gentleman. I confess, I fear for his safety. There appears to be a very small, dark discolouration at the bottom end of the cane. I should be able to determine whether it is in fact, blood, by a test that I myself invented in the course of my researches at the hospital. I shall perform the test immediately." Holmes got out of his chair and went over to the laboratory bench at one end of the living room.

"I presume he will wish to retrieve the cane," I mused.

"Undoubtedly," said Holmes, from the corner of the room. "He will return. And when he does, he should be able to tell us exactly where he found the cane and possibly shed some light on the matter."

As if on cue the bell downstairs rang out. A moment later I could hear the ex-client conversing with Mrs. Hudson, who appeared slightly uncertain as she showed him in to us for the second time.

"My cane," said the man. "I left it."

"You did indeed," said Holmes, coming up to him. "If you could possibly tell me where and when you found the cane, I would be grateful."

"Oh," said the man. "I had assumed that the cane had been thrown away. It did not have the appearance of lost property."

"You made no attempt to trace the owner."

"No. Look here, is this really any of your business?" asked the man.

"If you could give me the exact location of where you found the cane, I would be most grateful," said Holmes, politely. "I have no interest in getting you into trouble of any sort."

"Well, if you must know, I found it by a road that runs off Stoke Poges Lane, about a month ago," said the man, after a pause.

"Stoke Poges Lane ...which is located, where?"

The man sighed. "It runs from near to Slough Railway station to Stoke Poges. If you go down Stoke Poges Lane, after about a mile there is another lane leading off to the left. It is grassy and gravelly, not a good road to be travelling along by carriage or trap, but good enough to walk down."

"Is it secluded?"

"Very."

I wondered what the man had been doing there, but decided not to ask.

"It is a short cut to Stoke Park," said the man, as if reading my thoughts. "Now, if you don't mind, I would be most grateful if I could have the cane back."

"We would like to buy it from you," said Holmes. "Would ten shillings be enough?"

"Well, yes," said the man, in a surprised tone. "Ten shillings would be more than enough."

Holmes produced the shillings and opened the door for the man, out of which he walked with his new-found wealth.

"Well, you have your information," I said. "Assuming that he was telling the truth."

"Some of it," said Holmes, walking over to his laboratory again. "There is more information to be had. I shall perform a fingerprint test of my own device." He got down a jar of white powder from which he proceeded to sprinkle the contents onto the cane. "Fingerprints are unique to the individual and techniques to show them up have been in existence for thirty years; yet the judicial system still deems them as inadmissible evidence. We live in very backward times, Watson, though I believe, not for much longer. The criminal has had his heyday and in the future will have to become extremely competent if he is to survive. Now, this is curious. There appear to be a set of fingerprints at the bottom end of the cane. Ah! And I also have the result of the blood test. Haemoglobin is present in the sample, indicating that it is in fact, blood."

"That does not necessarily indicate anything sinister," I said.

"No," replied Holmes. "But when coupled with the fact that a gentleman named Arthur Trenthill, of independent means, who was known to drink at the Old Crown Hotel in Slough, has been missing for a week, it becomes of a sinister nature.

"How on earth do you know that?"

"Unlike you, Watson, I do not read The Times newspaper from cover to cover on a daily basis. I confine my attention to the articles reporting crime, and the agony column. In this way I am able to remember everything I read, for my memory is not cluttered with information that is irrelevant to my work."

This I could well believe, for in the past I had found that Holmes' knowledge in certain areas was astoundingly weak.

"Well, it still doesn't mean anything," I continued to object. "Arthur Trenthill might have had an accident, drawing blood in the process, which then got onto the cane."

"But why would he leave his cane in the lane?"

"Well, there could be many reasons why he would leave the cane in the lane. Maybe he had taken a dislike to it and wished to throw it away. Or maybe he stopped for a rest and left it there by mistake."

"Possibly," said Holmes. "In order to find out more we would need to examine the area where the cane was found."

"You mean we should travel down to Slough and go and have a look around that spot in Stoke Poges Lane?"

"Precisely, Watson. You may be interested to know that there have recently been reports of muggings in the area. Two weeks ago, there was a report in the newspaper that a gentleman was attacked near Dorney by a masked man and robbed of his belongings. Dorney is, I believe, in the vicinity of Slough."

"And you think that this event might be connected with the gentleman's disappearance?"

"I do not think anything. I wish to establish the facts."

"You are not in the pay of a client."

"Nor am I in need of it. I am not as financially insecure as I was when we first met. Some of my clients have been of an affluent disposition and were extremely generous in their payment for my services. I am now in a position to investigate whichever case is of interest me without consideration of its potential remuneration. I would be most grateful if you would accompany me to Slough this afternoon."

"Today?"

"That is, if you have nothing else to do."

"I have had no urgent call-outs as yet."

"Excellent. Then we shall proceed to Paddington station as soon as you are ready. However, I wish to purchase a small, lockable casket on the way."

I did not ask why. It was typical of Holmes to move in a mysterious way and I did not weary myself in asking him to explain in graphic detail every turn of his actions.

"Oh, and another thing. It might be profitable for us to stay for a night or two at the Old Crown Hotel as that was the place where Arthur Trenthill was last seen. We shall be posing as travellers on our way from London to Penzance."

"Right you are, Holmes," I said, and went into my room to pack. My experience in Afghanistan had trained me to be up and ready within minutes. Holmes was equally quick. In no time at all we were out of the front door and on our way to Baker Street underground station.

We arrived at Paddington station at one o'clock in the afternoon and caught what was to be a direct, non-stopping service to Slough that would arrive within the hour. This it did; once off the train, Holmes bought a guide book from a station stall. Outside, a line of cabs awaited the train passengers but Holmes walked on past them, towards the crossroads of the Bath Road and Slough High Street. Here stood four coaching inns, a remnant from the past, the Old Crown Hotel being the most prominent. It was strange to think that fifty years previously, the bustling High Street in which we now stood would have been an empty road, passing through a picturesque village, the quietude broken only by the occasional stage coach thundering along on its way from London and rattling to a stop at the coaching inns. The Old Crown Hotel seemed most respectable. We went up to the reception, whereupon we were greeted by a dutiful lackey.

"Yes, we do have rooms," he said, in response to our enquiry. "If you will just sign the guest book." Holmes took the pen and wrote his name as George Tregellan of an address in Penzance. I wrote the first name that came into my head and an address in London.

"I have some valuable items that I would like to be

locked away during our stay," said Holmes, producing the little casket that he had bought on our journey. "Is there anything that you can offer me?"

"I can put it in our office safe," said the lackey.

"That will do admirably," said Holmes, placing the casket upon the counter.

"I'm afraid the footman is not available to carry your bags," said the lackey. "It is his afternoon off." We were left to find our own way up to our rooms, which were situated at the front, looking out onto the High Street. They were most comfortable, with heavy curtains and antique armchairs, into one of which Holmes immediately sank. He opened his guide book and consulted it.

"It would be interesting to visit Stoke Poges," said Holmes. "According to this book it is full of history and grand residences. We can investigate that other little matter on the way."

I had been under the impression that the other little matter had been the sole reason for our visit but fell in with Holmes' tourist mode.

"I have to admit, this whole area is full of history and has a distinct atmosphere of antiquity," I said.

"Quite so," said Holmes. "We are close to a place known as Maidenhead Thicket, once notorious for highwaymen, owing to the large number of coaches that would pass through it and the vast amount of cover that was provided by trees on either side of the road. According to this guidebook, one of the most famous highwaymen, by name of Claude Duval was reputed to have frequented 'The Black Boy', situated on the other side of the crossroads from here."

"How fascinating," I said. "Although I doubt that we

will ever have any means of ascertaining the truth of the claim."

"Well, we are here to investigate a different matter," said Holmes. "Shall we go?"

I stood up in readiness. We sauntered out of the Old Crown Hotel with Holmes ostentatiously waving his guide book. A little way along the Bath Road, Stoke Poges Lane led off northwards. On either side of the lane were rows of trees with farmland and wooded areas behind them.

About a mile on, a grassy, gravelly road leading off to the left appeared. We advanced along it, noting how quiet, green and shady everything was. About a quarter of a mile along was a piece of coarse sacking lying in the road beside the trees. When we reached it, Holmes picked it up and held it in front of me without a word. I then saw that there were some markings in the muddy ground just beyond the trees; footprints running in two opposite directions and a track beside them; it was a long, wide, shallow track that led towards a clump of trees. Holmes turned to look.

"It rained ten days ago," he said. "These imprints are less than ten days old." He then got out his tape and began to measure the depth and other dimensions of the prints. We then went off following the track into the trees and came across the body of a man stretched out upon the undergrowth. Judging from the general appearance of the body, I estimated that the man had been dead for a week. There was a cut on his forehead and evidence of extensive bruising upon his face and neck.

"The work of a mugger, I suppose," I said. "I suspect he will no longer have his money or pocket watch upon him."

"He was obviously dragged here, hence the shallow track," said Holmes, as he reconstructed the action in his usual fashion. "Judging from his shoes, these footprints are not his. They are those of the mugger. The latter must have been following him up the road behind the cover of the trees and then jumped out at him. There was a struggle, in which the gentleman pulled the sacking off from the mugger's face. In fear of being identified, the mugger then took the step of silencing him for ever. To increase the length of time before the murder was discovered, he dragged the body to this spot. He then fled the scene, as can be observed from the returning footprints."

"Should we inform the police?" I asked.

"We shall have to," said Holmes. "Though what actual good that will do, I can't imagine. No doubt the local police have already tried to find the man responsible for the Dorney assault."

"Then we cannot disturb the body," said I. "It will be difficult for me to examine it thoroughly."

"We can, however, examine his hat," said Holmes, picking up the bowler that lay discarded by the body. "A great deal can be deduced from a hat, perhaps even more than from a coroner's report. The initials, 'A.T.', are immediately visible in the lining, strongly suggesting that we have found the missing Arthur Trenthill. I can also deduce that he has no valet; the hat has not been brushed for a very long time. This is in accordance with his boots, which have not been polished at all recently."

"How did he come to be walking along here in the first place?" I asked.

"According to this map, Stoke Poges Manor lies at

the end of this lane," said Holmes. "He may have had connections there."

"Well, he is certainly dressed as a gentleman," I said.

"I suggest that we go back to the Old Crown and take refreshment there," said Holmes. "That is, after we have called in at the police station."

When we arrived back at the Old Crown, Holmes appeared to lose his way and ended up coming into the building via a back courtyard that was covered in muddy footprints, including our own. We scraped the mud off our feet on the boot scraper at the back door and stepped in. On our way to the stairs, we passed the door to the lounge. It was half open; Holmes walked through and I followed him. There were no guests present in the large, elegant room apart from a countrified gentleman, who sat in an armchair in the corner near the fire, in an apparently distraught state. He was being attended to in a most sympathetic manner by a footman-cum-ostler, who was offering him the hotel's best brandy, on the house. The latter was a young man, fit and athletic, with an expression of daring about him.

"I think I was lucky to escape with my life," the gentleman was saying. "Had I not had a gold watch and twenty pounds in my possession, I believe the ruffian would have made an attack on my person. In future, I shall never leave the house with less than twenty pounds."

"Very sensible, if I may say so, sir," said the footman. "If I were in your shoes, I would do exactly the same." He poured the recovering guest another glass of brandy and continued to stand in attendance.

"Thank you very much, young man," said the guest.

"You are a credit to this hotel. What is your name, may I ask?"

"John, sir. John Thomas."

"No, no, your real name, not the name given to every footman up and down the country."

"Davill, sir. John Davill."

"Well, Davill, would you be able to run a couple of errands for me tomorrow afternoon?"

"I'm afraid not, sir. Tomorrow is my day off. I have promised to visit my aunt in Windsor."

"Day off? I thought you had already had an afternoon off this afternoon."

"Yes, sir. I have one afternoon off a week, and one Sunday off a month. Tomorrow is such a Sunday."

"It sounds almost reasonable when you put it like that," said the gentleman. "Never mind. I shall put in a good word for you, when I leave."

"Thank you, sir" said the footman. "I hope you are feeling a lot better, now."

"Oh, I am, I am," said the man. He now appeared sufficiently recovered to become aware of his surroundings, and turned momentarily towards us.

"Oh, good evening, gentlemen," he said. "I am sorry. I did not see you there. What will you think of me. I just had a most unfortunate experience on the road a little way from here. I was walking towards Salt Hill, when I was set upon by a masked man. He stole all items of value that I had upon my person then made off through the trees."

"You say he was masked," said Holmes.

"Yes, sir," said the gentleman. "Of his face, I saw nothing. It was covered in a sack with holes for him to see through. He was armed with a bludgeon. I don't mind admitting, I was fairly terrified. However, I feel a lot better now."

"I am glad to hear it," said Holmes. "We shall have to take extra care ourselves, shall we not, Butler. Why, not an hour ago, we ourselves were walking around the countryside that surrounds this town, and had no less than fifty pounds upon us, in total. No doubt that would have saved us from physical harm, but we can do without losing fifty pounds."

"If it saves me from grievous bodily harm, I would gladly lose a thousand," said I.

"Quite so," said the gentleman. "I'm sorry, gentlemen, we have not been introduced. I am John Reginald, of Albatross Grange in Ashwell, Hertfordshire."

"Mr. George Tregellan and Mr. James Butler, at your service," said Holmes.

"And how do you come to be in the market town of Slough?" asked Mr. Reginald.

"We are on our way back to my home in Penzance," said Holmes. "The entire journey is twelve hours, a period that for me, is too long to be sitting in one place. I and my friend are doing the journey in stages at our leisure, stopping off to see all the historic attractions that lie on the way."

"Oh, I see," said Mr. Reginald. "Did you start from London?"

"Yes," replied Holmes. "I came up to London in order to collect some gold ingots from a bank."

"Gold? Now there is a sound investment," said Mr. Reginald. "You cannot go wrong with gold."

"Precisely what I thought when I purchased them,"

replied Holmes. "The only drawback is that unlike stocks and shares, they are a tangible asset. When I get to Penzance, I intend to deposit them into another bank. At the moment, they are in the safekeeping of the hotel."

"Well, as long as you do not walk around with them on your person, I should think that they will be safe enough," muttered Mr. Reginald.

"Of course," said Holmes. "I do not intend to wander along lonely country roads with them. At each stage of the journey they shall be deposited in a safe."

"How long will you be staying in Slough?"

"Oh, I think we have seen all that there is to see in Slough. We shall be travelling on to Bath tomorrow."

"By train, I presume?"

"Yes," replied Holmes.

"Well, you could be in for a lengthy journey," said Mr. Reginald. "There are rail works taking place this weekend between Maidenhead and Reading. The trains won't be running again until Monday."

"Oh," said Holmes. "That is a nuisance. I particularly wanted to be in Bath by tomorrow evening."

"You could always take a coach between Maidenhead and Reading," suggested Mr. Reginald. "In fact, the Great Western Railway Company may even be laying on coaches for the passengers for that stretch."

"I doubt it," said Holmes. "And even if they were, I would much prefer to travel by my own coach. Yes, I believe that that is what we shall do. We shall hire a coach from Maidenhead to Reading. It cannot be more than ten miles. Thank you, Mr. Reginald for informing me in advance of the problem. I am most grateful."

"Glad to be of service," said Mr. Reginald.

"Would you be requiring any refreshment?" the footman enquired of us.

"Yes, indeed," said Holmes. To my surprise, he ordered a glass of sherry. I asked for the same.

"Are you sure it is a good idea for us to be travelling through Maidenhead Thicket by hired coach?" I objected. "What about those highwaymen you were talking about?"

"That was a hundred years ago, Butler," said Holmes. "There are no longer any highwaymen, nor in fact, is there a thicket. The last highway robbery to take place in England was in 1801."

With lightning efficiency the footman appeared again, with two glasses of sherry on a tray. "Will you be requiring dinner this evening?" he asked, as he placed them upon the table before us.

"Yes," said Holmes. "Please reserve us two places in the dining room. We shall go to our rooms to change." He stood up and left the room, carrying one of the glasses. I followed him upstairs with mine. Once in our rooms, Holmes closed the door and placed the sherry glass upon the table. He then produced the home-made fingerprinting 'kit' that he had designed himself. I watched as he poured the sherry away, dusted the glass with powder and peeled off the print on a piece of tape. He then compared the impression with that on another tape that he had brought with him, staring intently at the two samples.

"I take it that you suspect the footman," I said.

"The fingerprints on this glass match those found on the end of the cane," said Holmes.

"Well, that is to be expected," I argued. "We know that Arthur Trenthill used to drink here. The footman was obviously handing him his cane. There is nothing incriminating about that whatsoever."

"Yes, except the prints on the cane were at its bottom end," said Holmes. "Normally when handing a guest their cane, the footman would not grasp it by that end."

"Well, I have to admit, that is a bit odd. But to have taken the sherry glass up here, you must have already suspected the footman," I persisted.

"His afternoons off coincide with the time of both the attack near Dorney and the one as described by Mr. Reginald in the lounge," said Holmes.

"Purely circumstantial," I said.

"There is much circumstantial evidence surrounding the footman," said Holmes. "While circumstantial evidence can and must never be used to convict a man, it certainly is enough to produce a suspect for the crime."

"What other circumstantial evidence is there?"

"The fact that the two men who were attacked are both known to have visited the Old Crown Hotel. That alone is highly significant."

"It is not highly significant," I said. "Just about anyone of means who visits Slough visits the Old Crown Hotel. It is the obvious place to go for accommodation or refreshment."

"There are also footprints," said Holmes. "The footprints that we found near the body were made by a man who weighed approximately a hundred and eighty pounds, as does the footman. The shoe size also matches that of the footman."

"How do you know that whoever created the footprints weighed a hundred and eighty pounds?"

"From the depth and surface area of the prints in

comparison with the depth and surface area of my own, made in the same place. I took measurements of both."

"Anything else?"

"The footprints found near the scene of the crime were identical to one set of those in the courtyard."

"Well, isn't that something," I retorted. "Half of England's work force wears outdoor boots of that kind. No, Holmes, none of the so-called evidence that you have put before me will do. Not even the fingerprints. Even if they were as incriminating as you believe, they would not be admissible in a court of law."

"Indeed," said Holmes. "However, I intend to produce a piece of evidence that no one will be able to dispute."

"What is that?"

"I would rather not say at present. I have a plan. Would it be too much trouble for you to assist me with it, without knowing the details? These walls have ears."

"As usual, of course, Holmes. Just tell me what to do."

"You are merely not to question my actions or anything that happens on our journey tomorrow. All will soon become clear." He put down the two pieces of tape. "Shall we go down to dinner?"

I considered this case to be one of the more relaxing ones, for it appeared that I would be allowed to eat and sleep. So often in other cases would I be woken at six in the morning by Holmes requiring my immediate assistance, or having my lunch interrupted by an urgent message summoning me to his side. I hoped that the relaxation would not be too much for Holmes, for he seemed to thrive on pressure; but at dinner, he showed another side of himself, a humorous, jolly side, of which I had only seen glimpses on previous occasions. The next day, however, he was back in his old form. He returned to the hotel as I was packing, having been out for some time early in the morning.

When we made ourselves known at the reception, the lackey placed the little casket in front of Holmes, who unzipped his case upon the counter and placed the casket within. We were then ready to leave. When we got to the station, it turned out that everything that Mr. Reginald had said was absolutely true. We were forced to get out of the train at Maidenhead and hire alternative transportation. This, Holmes appeared to have already arranged, although I at the time I was not sure how; our coach was waiting for us outside the station. The coachman nodded to Holmes in a familiar sort of way and we lost no time in getting inside and taking off down the road to Reading. Holmes kept the case containing the casket in the interior of the coach by his side. We had not progressed more than a mile before the coach came to an abrupt stop and two burly men got in, both of whom appeared to be known to Holmes. They would not converse with us but sat opposite us with their arms folded. It did not seem appropriate that I should ask them any questions.

Holmes had not been entirely correct that there was no longer a thicket at Maidenhead; the road had now become a narrow path with a good amount of trees bending over from either side, forming an arch under which we were passing. The rattling of the coach seemed louder in such a quiet place, drowning out the wind and bird calls. We could not have been progressing at more than three miles per hour along the gravelly surface. After about ten minutes, the coach came to a stop. The window was let down and what looked like a pistol suddenly appeared in my face. A second later, however, it disappeared.

I leant out of the window to see the coachman grappling with a hefty man who was masked by a piece of sacking. The other two men were already out of the coach and between the three of them they appeared to have no trouble in overcoming the perpetrator of the crime; as the handcuffs closed about his wrists and ankles, he fell to the ground. Holmes pulled away the sack which covered his face to reveal the footman of the hotel. It was as my friend had suspected.

"No doubt you would have been greatly sympathetic towards me on account of my ordeal, had I returned to the hotel," said Holmes. "Drawing on your employer's brandy reserves to provide consolation. You were very convincing."

"Who are you?" asked the footman, in a low voice.

"You are correct in thinking that I am not George Tregellan of Penzance. I am a consulting detective by name of Sherlock Holmes. I am afraid you left too many traces behind you in your escapades."

"We are indebted to you, Mr. Holmes," said one of the men who had mysteriously joined us on our journey. "Had you not informed us of developments it would have been another fortnight before we had the case wrapped up. I am sure that if the property stolen from the victims can be recovered, you will be well-recompensed."

"You were lucky that I was not overly occupied," said Holmes. "My diary has become increasingly full of late, owning to a high success rate."

The footman was roughly bundled into the coach and they all got back in again, save Holmes.

"Let us walk back to Maidenhead," Holmes called out to the coachman. "I do not relish travelling with a desperate man." The coachman turned the coach around and it trundled off again, through the trees. A moment later, Holmes and I followed on.

"You remember he said that his name was Davill," I said, as we progressed. "A possible adulteration of the name 'Du Vall', that of the notorious highwayman who according to your guidebook was reputed to drink at the Black Boy. Could it be ..."

"I do not consider that question worthy of investigation," said Holmes. "However, no self-respecting highwayman would lead the life of a monk. Doubtless the entire region is littered with descendants of his illegitimate children. I presume you will make something of the issue in your embellished report of the case."

"Were it not for the embellishments, the public would not read your work," I said. "When you finally come to writing up one of your cases yourself, you will realize that your audience is not interested in scientific papers. I am popularizing your work."

The Light Bringer

It was about midday when I returned from the East End of London, in a state of shock that had been unknown to me since my experiences as a doctor in Afghanistan. Not since then had I seen such horror, despite the fact that I had been to that part of London before. Owing to my limited experience in Afghanistan, I had been asked to accompany a colleague to visit a street full of patients, all of whom were ailing from the same terrible sickness – I had attempted to find an alternative diagnosis, but could only agree that what we were witnessing was a repeat epidemic of the plague, which had supposedly been extinct since the eighteenth century. Fortunately, the epidemic appeared to be localized to one small area. The patients that I saw were not covered in buboes, as I had expected but had generally only one or two and always in the same two places. The survival rate, the doctor whom I was accompanying told me, was thirty-five per cent, an improvement on the twenty-five per cent that had been the case in the seventeenth century. Usually, I try not to think about catching diseases off my patients, but this time, I kept my distance. There were no rats in the yards behind the houses, for they had all been killed in an attempt to control the spread of the disease.

"There has been a case reported in Southend," the doctor whom I was with told me. "Most peculiar. He is known to be a relation of the patient in the house we were last at. The rat fleas must have been transferred to him on a visit from his relative."

I could add nothing to his knowledge. My time in Afghanistan had given me a working knowledge of typhoid and malaria, but there had been no cases of plague. I told the doctor this, and he said he was glad that I had come anyway, for he could not stand the horror alone. It seemed strange that such a disease could suddenly reawaken in our modern, scientifically advanced times.

"I presume they will not be marking the doors of the plague victims and locking them inside, together with their healthy relatives," I said.

"It would not work if they did," said the doctor. "It did not work then, and it would not work now. No, the disease is transmitted by rat fleas; that much was proven by Doctor Yersin five years ago in the course of his studies in Hong Kong. This epidemic originated around there and arrived here on a ship."

I dared not question his authority, for as a medical man, he was my senior. His explanations all sounded reasonable enough. At Whitechapel, we parted company, and I made my way back to civilization as quickly as possible on the London Underground, whilst he took his carriage that had stood ostentatiously waiting for him at the outreaches of the East End. As the train moved off, the nervous state to which I was unaccustomed began to wear off. By the time I got to Baker Street, it was gone, and I was feeling quite myself again.

I went up to the doors of 221B Baker Street and let myself in. Walking up the stairs, I passed Mrs. Hudson on the landing. "There is a client there, at the moment," she said. "Holmes was disappointed that you were not here. However, no doubt he will fill you in on the details."

In view of this information, I knocked on the sitting-room door. It was opened by Holmes, who beckoned me to sit down near a very important-looking gentleman who turned out to be the Governor of the Bank of England.

"This is Dr. Watson, to whom you may say anything that you would say to me," said Holmes.

"So I have heard," said the Governor. "However, I will not repeat myself. Well, Mr. Holmes, I have told you the facts. What do you suggest I do about these forged notes?"

"Do you have an example of the forgeries?" asked Holmes.

"Indeed I do," said the Governor, producing from his pocket two large, white notes, which were evidently fivers. He handed them to Holmes, who held them up to the light and then took them over to his laboratory, where he examined them with various magnifiers.

"Well, you are quite right," said Holmes. "The forgery has been perfectly executed. I can see no difference between these two notes, and would not know which was the original and which was the forgery. The only thing that would make me aware that one is forged is the fact that they both have the same serial number."

"Indeed," said the Governor. "We have estimated that there exists one of these forgeries for every three genuine five pound notes. The market is flooded with them and as a result, we are going into hyperinflation. Our economy is on the brink of ruin. Which brings me to another question: who is responsible for the forgeries? Their quality and quantity demonstrate that they cannot be the work of a common criminal."

"No, they are not," said Holmes. "I suspect that they are the work of a higher, possibly foreign organization, one that aims to destroy the nation rather than to fill its own pockets."

"I am also inclined to that opinion," said the Governor. "But what is this foreign organization?"

"I have an idea," said Holmes. "However, I would rather not reveal it until I am certain."

"Well, in the meantime, how do we stop them?"

Holmes put down the notes. "The counterfeiters are so adept in their manufacturing that I fear any attempt to make the notes forge-proof will be to no avail. The only way to thwart them is to speed up the rate at which the forgeries are removed from the system. May I ask how the numbers on the notes are recorded when deposited into the bank?"

"They are copied by hand into a ledger book."

"Too time consuming. Now if you were to print the serial number a third time in one corner of the note, this could be torn off and stuck into the ledger. That should speed things up considerably."

"The committee may want to consider this approach," said the Governor. "I suppose an increase in staff would also be advisable."

"Indeed," said Holmes. "Threefold at least. You might also like to consider printing random serial numbers, so that only the bank knows which numbers are genuine."

"That we have done in the past," said the Governor. "And I have to say that under the current circumstances, it is a more secure method."

"Is it just five pound notes or is it other denominations as well?"

"It is all denominations. However, nothing has as yet been done to the coinage. That is, nothing on this level of professionalism."

"That is just as well," said Holmes. "For it is much harder to remove counterfeit coins from circulation than counterfeit notes. However, the problem is not yet completely solved. I am sorry I cannot be of more help but I feel you are up against powers that are at least equal to my own."

"Really," said the Governor, putting the notes away again. "Well, you have already given me hope. I shall put your suggestions to the committee without delay. I really am most grateful. And now, as I assume you are equally busy, I shall take my leave. You will not be disconcerted, I trust, should I call again. Goodbye, Mr. Holmes ... Dr. Watson." And he stood up with renewed vigour and left the room.

"Well," I said when he had gone. "It would appear that you are of high profile in the public world."

"I would like to think that I am changing history," said Holmes. "That was what I was put here to do."

I was about to make some reference to his modesty, when he asked me: "How did you get on in the East End?"

"Oh, Holmes, don't remind me," I said. "It was terrible. You will not believe this, but there really does seem to be an epidemic of bubonic plague erupting in the area. All the symptoms are there; I saw it for myself. Mr. Hounslow and I went round the entire street where it appears to have currently confined itself, save for one isolated case in Southend. The doctor couldn't understand that. He said that the plague must have travelled to Southend by fleas."

"It is not like a doctor to say he cannot understand something," said Holmes. "Did he give any explanation as to where the epidemic came from?"

"He thinks it came by ship from Asia or the Far East," I said.

"And you, Watson," said Holmes. "What do you think?"

"I presume that it did. There is, after all, an epidemic of bubonic plague raging through China and India as we speak. It has recently been proven beyond all scientific doubt that bubonic plague is transmitted by rat fleas. I have seen the article about it in The Lancet."

"No doubt you have," said Holmes. "And yet, I feel that this epidemic is not a natural disaster. Everything about it has the vibes of Professor Moriarty, as does the current deluge of forged bank notes into our currency."

I paused before I spoke again. Finally, I said, "Are you referring to the Professor Moriarty who fell into the chasm at the Reichenbach Falls, bounced off a rock, and ended up in the water?"

"I am indeed, Watson. It later occurred to me that the man who fell into the chasm could have been anyone – how do I know that it was Moriarty? I had only met him on one occasion prior to our encounter in Switzerland; a few days before this encounter a man presenting himself as Professor Moriarty came to my rooms; I am now in doubt as to the identity of that man."

"But this is pure speculation, Holmes," I argued. "There has been no sign of Professor Moriarty for eight years."

"So did I also think," said Holmes. "But on reflection, there were one or two affairs that have occurred in the last few years that had the hallmark of his work."

"You are overworked," I said. "Stop thinking about Moriarty and I am sure you will soon feel better."

"I wish I could," said Holmes. "And probably would, were it not for the letter that was delivered by hand this morning." He walked over to the writing table and picked up the communication.

"What is it?" I asked.

Holmes held it out to me. The letter was written on the most expensive notepaper possible and ran as below:

Mr. Sherlock Holmes

We allegedly last met at the Reichenbach Falls in Switzerland, resulting in my ultimate demise. However, contrary to what you may believe, we have never met. If you and I were characters in a novel, it might be considered poetic that we should eventually meet; however, in reality, if you believe that you will ever see me in the flesh, you are living in a world of fantasy. The gentleman who came to see you at your rooms in Baker Street was not me, but an associate of mine. His name was Dr. Hans Friedholm, a mathematician, albeit a very poor one. His loyalty, however, was a different matter. I had no hesitation in engaging him in the task of despatching you from this planet. Imagine my dismay when I witnessed him tumbling into the chasm, when it should have been either you or the two of you together. He had provided me with a demonstration of his surprising physical strength; I had not, however, verified his statement that he was well-versed in the martial art of baritsu. Judging from his performance in unarmed combat against you, I realize that this was a gross exaggeration.

I now serve a higher authority; should you interfere it is they who shall deal with you, not me. I therefore urge you to resist the temptation of thwarting me in my work, the nature of which I am sure you are already aware.

M

"Good Heavens, Holmes," I said. "It certainly doesn't look like a forged letter. What does he mean by, 'I now serve a higher authority?'

"Have you ever heard of the Illuminati?" asked Holmes.

"Are they not a secret society rumoured to control world affairs by masterminding events?"

"Indeed," said Holmes. "Their aim is to rule the world. In order to do this they must first break up every nation. Moriarty hopes to join them but at the moment he is on trial. He is worried that I will stymie his career. And he is right to be worried."

"But he says that the 'authority' will deal with you if you don't back off," I cried, in alarm.

"If the Illuminati wished to do away with me, they would have already done so," said Holmes. "He is merely trying to intimidate me. And now that he is working for them he will not take action against me himself."

"It does not sound as though he is in a strong position," I said.

"He is not; and he knows it. That is why he has written to me. If it were not for me, his place within the 'authority' would be a foregone conclusion. Now it is in the balance."

"Do you think that the Illuminati will succeed in their plan to destroy the nation?"

"Well, if they do, it will be the first time that they have ever been completely successful," said Holmes. "The Illuminati have existed in some form or other for over two thousand years. They have already made several attempts in the past to wipe Europe from the map, using similar methods. It was they who were responsible for the Black Death which raged through Europe in the fourteenth century and returned as the Great Plague in the seventeenth century. On both occasions the plague wiped out half of the population of Britain and on both occasions, the population recovered. There are at present, three or four times as many people in the Britain as there were a hundred years ago, owing to the factories that have sprung up all over the country during the course of this century. The Illuminati is intent on removing what they regard as the surplus population."

"How can you be so sure that it is the Illuminati who are responsible for the plague in the East End?"

"Plague is their most powerful weapon," said Holmes. "They created it and have now, most probably, modified it so that it will spread more easily. It must be stopped at once, before the epidemic becomes a pandemic."

"What do you suggest?" I asked. "Should the entire East End be cordoned off?"

"An effective but inhumane method," said Holmes. "It would most probably prevent an outbreak through the entire land. However, I cannot have it on my conscience that someone within that unfortunate quarter who had the means and motivation to leave could not. No, we shall have to find an alternative method."

"Such as?"

"You are the doctor, Watson. What do you propose?"

As a doctor, I was more used to treating illness than preventing it; however, I gave the problem my undivided attention.

"Well, let me summarize what we know," I said. "In the mid-seventeenth century, bubonic plague was carried by rats and transmitted from them to humans by fleas. However, by the end of the century, the plague had mysteriously disappeared. What was the reason for this, I do not know."

"Quite," said Holmes. "Within that reason lies the key. If we can uncover the reason, we may be able to stop the epidemic dead in its tracks."

"Maybe it will not get beyond the East End, in any case."

"Don't you believe it. As I said, this epidemic has been purposely created with the express intention that it should break out all over England. There is not much time to be lost."

"What shall we do?"

"We shall pay a visit to Arthur Hallgood, an amateur historian, who has formed many theories on unsolved historical mysteries, including the disappearance of the plague. I knew the man personally, for he was at the University with me; like me, he never took a degree, for he preferred to go his own way in his studies. At the time when he should have been following the curriculum, he was writing a book concerning his theories which was published before he left the University. It was reviewed by several eminent historians, including his own tutor; to say that the reviews were unfavourable would be an understatement. They were the most damning and ridiculing reviews ever to have been received by a history book. Very soon, the book was out of print."

"Did you ever read the book?"

"No, I did not. It did not seem relevant to my work. However, I spoke to Hallgood about it on two occasions: on both these occasions, he told me that he was one hundred per cent certain that the theories in his book were correct. Those theories of which he was less certain, he had left out."

"Well, he seems pretty sure of himself, you can say that for him," I said.

"The self-assurance may be justified. In order to earn such incredible hostility from professional historians, the theories must have had some truth in them. Presumably his theories were in direct contradiction to theirs and so they could not afford to support them."

"Well, I suppose there is no harm in asking his opinion," I said.

"Can you be ready in ten minutes, Watson?" asked Holmes.

"Yes, Holmes," I said, as I always did, in these

circumstances. "Where does he live?"

"In Bloomsbury," said Holmes. "As you might expect."

"Is he a close friend of yours, this Arthur Hallgood?" I asked, as we speeded towards Bloomsbury in a hansom cab.

"No, not close," said Holmes. "However, he was one of the few people whom I knew at the University. He himself did not have many friends; he was regarded as something of a maverick. However, I found everything that he said to me to be perfectly logical."

I had to admit to myself that I was not entirely convinced as to the accuracy of Hallgood's theories; but this was purely prejudice, for I had as yet not heard any of them and was judging my opinion solely on the fact that they had been rejected by eminent historians. Being a professional myself, I was reluctant to criticize the professionalism of others.

We arrived at the house in Bloomsbury where Holmes believed that Hallgood was currently living. The building was impressive and had obviously once been a town house owned by one of the upper ten thousand. It had, however, been converted into flats, which I had to admit was a shame in a way. It appeared that we were in luck: Hallgood's name was clearly printed next to the uppermost doorbell. Holmes rang it and after a short while, the door opened. An ageless sort of man who appeared fairly ordinary but for the glint in his eye stood before us.

"Holmes," he exclaimed. "I was wondering if I would ever see you again."

"You haven't changed," said Holmes. "This is my friend and colleague, Dr. Watson. This is not a social call.

We have a matter of importance which we would like to discuss with you, that is, if you are not immediately engaged in something else."

"Yes, of course," said the man. "Come upstairs."

We followed him up the wide, elegant staircase that had been lavishly built a hundred years ago, and stepped into his chambers. They were shockingly untidy, even more untidy than Holmes' lodgings for the floor was covered in a disarray of papers.

"I see you are still very much a historian," said Holmes, noting the evidence for this.

"Oh, indeed," said Hallgood. "Nothing else is of any interest to me. I believe I know more about history than any man alive."

"That is precisely why we are here," said Holmes. "You may be aware that there is currently a plague epidemic in the East End of London that threatens to expand into the rest of the country if nothing is done. As this appears to be a case of history repeating itself, we would like to hear your thoughts on the matter."

"Yes, I am aware of it," said Hallgood. "The epidemic started with a single case in Cranbrook Street which was immediately followed by two further cases in the houses opposite. It is believed that these cases were the result of transmission of the bacteria from rats to humans and that these rats were transported to the East End of London by ships from India and the Far East. However, I do not favour that theory."

"Why not?"

"Because ... I'm sorry, would you like to sit down? You will excuse the mess." Hallgood quickly removed the books and papers that covered the chairs beside us and we finally sat down. Hallgood himself remained standing.

"Would you like a drink?" he asked. I wondered if he was very unused to company.

"Do not trouble yourself, Hallgood," said Holmes. "If you could just tell us what you think is the cause of the epidemic, and more importantly, how it can be stopped."

"Very well," said Hallgood. "It has nothing whatsoever to do with rats. It is due to a haemorrhagic virus that is being transmitted from person to person; the same virus that caused the Great Plague two hundred and fifty years ago."

"Oh, surely not," I said. "You are flying in the face of science. I have read the latest research on bubonic plague and know for a fact that it is caused by a bacterium, not a virus."

"Bubonic plague is indeed caused by a bacterium," said Hallgood. "But the plague with which we are dealing is not bubonic plague. It is something quite different. A few of the symptoms are similar, but on the whole, they are not. That was also the case with the plague in the seventeenth century."

"So you are saying that the Great Plague was not bubonic plague," I said, rather acidly.

"That is exactly what I am saying," said Hallgood. "All the evidence indicates this."

"But I saw the buboes for myself," I went on. "In the armpit and groin."

"Indeed," said Hallgood. "But had it been bubonic plague, there would have been buboes in other places as well."

"It appears that you are branching out from history

and are now entering the realms of medicine and detection," said Holmes. "Our very professions, to be precise."

"Oh, I do not mean to encroach on your territory," said Hallgood. "But academic areas have a habit of overlapping. I cannot help that."

"Well, your conclusions could be right," said Holmes. "There was, after all, a case in Southend. Your theory would explain that."

Hallgood nodded. "The virus has an incubation time of three weeks," he said. "For that reason, the means of transmission may go undetected for some time."

"They are at present killing all the rats, by order of the authorities," I said. "But if what you say is true, it won't make a scrap of difference."

"I am afraid not," said Hallgood.

"How do you think the epidemic started?" asked Holmes.

Hallgood suddenly went very serious. "As I said before, I do not believe it came off a ship from India or the Far East." He lowered his voice as though in fear of being overheard. "I am not certain, but I have a suspicion that it may have been deliberately introduced, right here in this country."

"Exactly what I thought," said Holmes. "I even know who by."

There was a silence, which I eventually broke.

"Deliberately introduced or not, how are we to stop it?" I asked. "And if we do, how do we prevent it from starting again?"

"We must inform the authorities as to the real means of transmission," said Holmes.

"They won't listen," I exclaimed. "They have it on the

authority of Mr. Hounslow that it is the rats that are spreading the plague."

"Then another expert witness must be called in to give an opposing opinion," said Holmes.

"Well, who?"

"You, my dear Watson."

"Me? You want me to put my reputation on the line?"

"Without your reputation, they will not listen to you."

"I doubt if they will listen to me with it, either. I am not that high up in the pecking order of doctors."

"Nevertheless, your opinion will carry some weight," said Holmes. "Unlike Hallgood's, which is demolished forever."

"Quite," said Hallgood. "I have no power whatsoever in this matter."

"But what if you're wrong?" I objected. "My reputation will also be demolished forever."

"Hallgood is certain that he is not wrong."

"I dare say he is. That does not mean that he is not wrong."

"If you are prepared to do a little independent research, you will find that the symptoms of bubonic plague and those of the current plague in the East End are widely different, with the exception of a few features," said Hallgood.

"Well, I have seen those afflicted for myself, so it should not be too difficult to verify that statement," I said. "However, I am still most reluctant to get involved. Were I to present this theory to the medical world and they rejected it, as they probably would, I could be struck off."

"Then we must go to the East End ourselves," said

Holmes, gravely. "And warn those who are as yet without symptoms not to come close to those who are. We shall take all precautions possible."

I had previously made up my mind never to return to the East End of London, but now felt compelled to comply with Holmes' wishes. Hallgood, however, said that he was a theoretical historian and could not bring himself to come. Holmes did not appear to expect him to. "Let us return to Baker Street and prepare for our expedition into the darkest corner of London. It could be that there is no danger, for we descend from those who survived the Great Plague, and might therefore be immune."

"I shall not be relying on that hypothesis," I said. "The last time that I was there, I stood well back from the patients."

The cab driver would take us no further than Stepney Green. "I 'opes you knows what yous is doing, Governors," he said, as we emerged from the cab.

"Here's half-a-crown," said Holmes. "Keep the change. The cab driver drove off immediately towards the West.

"Cranbrook Street is the infected area," I said. "I do not believe that the plague has as yet got any further. I can't believe I am here for the second time in one day." We walked on, past the rows of narrow terraced houses teeming with poverty-stricken people who nevertheless did not appear downtrodden. "It's the next street," I said to Holmes. As we walked along, a woman wearing a shabby, white apron suddenly obstructed our path.

"Come this way, doctor," she said. "My son has the plague. I am sure of it. He is deadly ill. You must come at once." She tugged my arm expectantly; we were lead down a narrow alleyway that ran between the houses, through a door and up a very narrow, steep staircase. In the back room upstairs, a young man lay upon a mattress on the floor, writhing and coughing.

"How long has he been ill?" I asked immediately.

"Two days," said she.

"He does not appear generally malnourished," I said. "That should increase his chances slightly. Do not let him become dehydrated, or too hot or too cold."

"I have been doing that," said she.

"Good. And do not allow any person to enter this room, other than a doctor or yourself. This plague is transmitted mainly by coughing."

"Coughing? But Dr. Hounslow in the next street said only this morning that it was rats. I have been killing all the rats in the back garden."

"I cannot comment on that. Could you tell me, have there been any other cases in this street?"

"No", said she. "You know, I am beginning to think he may have caught it off a woman in Cranbrook Street. He said she was coughing on the day he last saw her. Although it was some time ago, that."

"How long ago was it?"

"Oh, I would say about two or three weeks."

"Then there is a good chance that that was where he caught it. I have been informed by a pioneering source that this plague has an incubation time of three weeks, meaning that it takes three weeks after catching the infection before any symptoms are experienced."

"I will tell everyone this," said the woman. "They will

listen to me. I have nursed several through typhoid and other illnesses."

"We shall do the same," said Holmes, who had stood by until now. "Watson, I shall take the even numbers of this street, you take the odd. I shall meet you back here in one hour." Holmes immediately left the sick man's room.

"I do not know if the neighbours will take any notice of your friend's advice," said the woman. "He is a stranger in these parts."

"He may not be as much of a stranger as you think," said I. "Have you heard of Sherlock Holmes?"

"Sherlock Holmes? The famous detective who lives in Baker Street?"

"None other."

"Then you must be Doctor Watson."

"I am."

"Well, I never," said she.

"However, he may not introduce himself by name," I went on. "He is apt to conceal his identity."

"It was a lucky chance, meeting you in the street," said she.

"Yes," said I. "Lucky for us, as well."

The young man on the mattress suddenly began coughing again. The woman immediately knelt by him and offered him water, which he succeeded in swallowing.

"I shall heed your advice, doctor," she said, without turning to me, as she held the glass. I left the room and went back out into the street again. Children were playing there, as normal. Some were barefoot, but most of them wore shoes. Who could tell if they were already infected. Halfway along the street, I could see Holmes knocking on one of the doors. Contrary to what many people believe, he has a most courteous way with women, and as the men all appeared to be out of the houses, it would seem that he would be successful in his mission. I went to the other end of the street and started at that end. The first door opened to reveal a woman similar to the one I had just left, and I began my expedition up the street.

When we arrived back at Stepney Green, there were no cabs waiting, so we walked on to Whitechapel and took the underground back to Baker Street. "Well," I said, as we sat amongst the passengers, "We have done all that we can. It is now in the hands of fate. I just hope that you haven't caught anything yourself, Holmes. Plague is not the only affliction known to that area."

"Do not concern yourself over me," said Holmes. "I believe I have a high resistance to infection."

"I hope so," said I. As the train sped on past King's Cross, the East End became a forgotten zone. By the time we got to Baker Street, with its shops and hansom cabs veering round the corners of the Georgian blocks, it was as though the place did not exist. Only the evening newspaper that Mrs. Hudson had as usual placed in the rack gave us any reminder of its horrors, and even then, only in a second-hand, abstracted kind of way. Baker Street now seemed like an absolute paradise; for two months I barely strayed from the place, leading a useless existence, with the newspapers giving me a vague, daily reminder that despite my present comfort, the plague could soon be wafting its way towards the centre of London. According to the reports, it had spread throughout the streets that lay in the vicinity of Cranbrook Street, but no further. Perhaps the people whom we had so ardently warned had listened, and remained in that area, confined to their houses. I had no intention of going there to find out. However, one morning, as I sat at the breakfast table comfortably positioned by the fire, an article at the bottom right corner of the front page of a newspaper brought me out of my stupor. It read as below:

'The epidemic of plague (I noted the absence of the word 'bubonic') that began in Cranbrook Street, Mile End, and spread throughout the immediate neighbourhood appears to be waning. There are now no more than five cases and at least half of those afflicted are expected to recover. Two months after it began, the epidemic is passing as mysteriously as it came. Mr. Hounslow, Chief Surgeon at the Royal Free Hospital, has described the disappearance of the plague as 'miraculous'.'

"It is a pity that there is no mention of you in the report," said Holmes. "It would have done wonders for your career."

"I gave up my career in order to assist you, as you well know," I said.

"Well, a boost in your prestige might have lent you the opportunity to set up practice again, this time in far more auspicious premises," said Holmes.

"I thought you did not want me to have a practice," I said. "You might like to know that I discovered your little scheme back in '94. It was you who put up the money to buy my practice at an extortionate price, was it not? So that I might move back into Baker Street again."

"Yes," said Holmes. "And I now feel that I acted against your interests. You need something more going on in your life than merely taking notes during my consultations and writing frivolous reports of my escapades. No, Watson, if you wish to set up practice again, by all means do so. With the money that I have accumulated in the last decade, we might even be able to set you up in Harley Street."

"No, it's quite all right, Holmes," I said. "When I sold my practice, it was because I no longer wished to be a doctor on a regular basis. Do not think ill of yourself for providing me with the opportunity of selling it."

"Then I am relieved of all guilt," said Holmes.

"What about Moriarty?" I asked. "He is presumably still at large."

"He has failed to reinstate the plague," replied Holmes. "What is more, the number of illicit banknotes in circulation has dropped considerably. I fear his chances of becoming one of the Illuminati are rapidly diminishing."

"Thanks to you," I said. "You have been the only thing to stand between him and world domination. Do you think that he will embark upon further enterprises?"

"We shall soon find out," said Holmes. "Though I believe he is running out of chances."

"Surely he will be given a third chance," said I. "I thought things always came in threes."

"People expect them to," said Holmes. "I, however, do not see why they should. I never thought I would say this, but I am weary of Moriarty. If only Inspector Lestrade would come by, as he did in the old days with the latest case that was baffling him. He is not a complete idiot, so whenever he was stumped, I knew that the case would be not be in the rudimentary category."

The door to the sitting room opened. "Inspector Lestrade to see you, Mr. Holmes," said Mrs. Hudson, showing in the man himself.

"Good Heavens," said I. "What a coincidence."

"Not really," said Holmes, trying not to laugh. "Lestrade informed me by telegram that he would be coming at exactly this time. Owing to his many previous visits, I am familiar with the tread of his footsteps on our stairs. Please sit down, Lestrade. I trust you have something of interest to tell me."

"Indeed," said Lestrade. "A death under suspicious circumstances has occurred. If I had not formed your acquaintance, I would have gone along with the suicide theory, but as you once criticized me for allowing murders to get past me undetected, I tend to be more careful these days."

"Please fill me in with the salient details," said Holmes, leaning back in his chair and putting his fingertips together.

"About two hours ago, the body of a man was found floating in the Thames," said Lestrade. "My colleagues are all of the opinion that the man jumped from one of the bridges, probably Waterloo Bridge. This is an alarmingly frequent occurrence, although it used to be more frequent. Under normal circumstances I would have agreed with this verdict."

"But there was a distinguishing feature about this particular suicide," said Holmes.

"Yes, indeed. I am no doctor, but I did see the body. There were signs that he did not fall from a high bridge onto water. All the buttons on his clothes were still there. In addition to this, he had no obvious bruises."

"No doubt this will come out at the inquest."

"Not necessarily. Suicides are normally treated in a prejudiced and unsympathetic way. However, I shall press the matter. Now, you will realize that I want to get a hold on this case as soon as possible, for every hour that passes after an incident could lead to a loss of clues."

"Could you describe this man in detail?" asked Holmes.

"Well, he was wearing a suit bought from an expensive outfitter. I could not have afforded such clothes. Pale blue eyes, grey hair, and quite tall and thin. Of Irish extraction, judging from his physiognomy. In his forties, I would say."

"Did no one see him jump from a bridge?"

"I have sent out a sergeant to make enquiries," said Lestrade. "But we are not sure of the exact time that he entered the water."

"And you found nothing on him to identify him?"

"Nothing, save this." Lestrade produced a black, waterlogged pocketbook with a pencil attached to it. "This was found on his person. It contains a lot of strange scribbling, partially obliterated by the water, of which I can make little sense." He held out the book for Holmes' perusal.

Holmes opened it carefully and appeared to find the contents amusing. "It would appear that Moriarty still has a passing interest in mathematics," he said. "Despite his resignation from his chair at one of the smaller universities."

"Moriarty?" echoed Lestrade. "You mean Professor Moriarty?"

"None other," said Holmes.

Lestrade's expression became weary and derogative.

"I remember that in the old days, you had a fixation for the professor, believing him to be a master criminal," he said. "Now, it is true, we did round up a large gang of criminals that were rumoured to be connected with him, but we never found evidence linking him to any crime. I remember, Inspector MacDonald went round to see him once, when the professor had his chair in mathematics. He found him to be an extremely pleasant, learned and talented man."

"Did it never occur to you to wonder why Professor Moriarty resigned from his chair?"

"No. I presume he wished to pursue another career."

"Then you will not be aware of the dark rumours that surrounded him at the time. It was as a result of these rumours that he was compelled to resign. He then left the university town and came down to London, where his criminal affairs flourished to such a degree that he amassed a vast fortune, without any crime ever being traced to him. Only his agents were caught."

"Why do you think that the suicide was Moriarty?"

"The suicide was a man of Irish extraction and mathematically inclined; that narrows the field considerably. He was also affluent, and in his forties. How many men of that description are there in the world? I doubt if you will find more than a handful. Moriarty is an Irish name; Professor Moriarty was at one time a mathematician; owing to his criminal activities he was affluent, enabling him to buy expensive suits; he would be in his forties by now. In addition to this, it was recently communicated to me that Moriarty was now in the service of the highest ranking international criminals. It may be they who are responsible for this murder."

"Murder? So you share my suspicions?"

"I see nothing wrong with your deductions."

"Will you assist further with the case?"

"I think not," said Holmes. "On this occasion you seem to be doing well enough yourself. I have the utmost confidence in you."

"Well, thank you, Mr. Holmes, although I'm sure you don't mean it ..."

"You have improved over the years, Lestrade, despite your frequent relapses. I have not been an ineffective assistant."

"No, Holmes, you have not. And if I had not improved over the years, I would be a very poor inspector. I was not promoted to the C.I.D. for nothing. It is all right for you, with nothing to do all day but muse over the facts of a case, but I have other duties: paperwork, instructing those below me, following orders from my superior. And I am not, I feel, as well rewarded financially as you are."

"Why don't you leave the force, then, and set up on your own?"

"Oh, others have done so, but with little success. You have been one of the lucky ones, Mr. Holmes," said Lestrade.

"As for this case, I shall hesitate to mention your ideas at the inquest, but it is useful to know your stance on things. It always turns out to have a grain of truth in it, although it doesn't seem like it at the time. Is there anything else that you can add?"

"No," said Holmes. "As I said, you are doing splendidly."

"Well, I will be on my way, then," said Lestrade.

"You won't stay for a cup of coffee?"

"No, I am eager to get back to the Yard and look into what you have told me," said Lestrade. "I will let you know of any further developments." He stood up and left, in a zealous fashion.

"Well, Lestrade seems to be going all out for it, these days," I said, after a while.

"Yes, as always," said Holmes. "He got to the rank of Detective Inspector through dogged determination. If there's a will, there's a way."

"That proverb did not apply to Moriarty," I said. "Assuming that the man in the river was him."

"Well, obviously, his will did not match mine," said Holmes. "Although his intellect did. He was, I suspect, the better mathematician."

I was about to dispute this, when a thought struck me.

"You wouldn't be Irish as well, would you by any chance?"

"That is for me to know and you to guess," answered Holmes.

221B Baker Street

"If it is my advice you want, I would suggest that you turn your buildings into an hotel," said Mr. Greengrass. I was sitting opposite him across his desk at the bank. For years he had been my financial adviser.

"An hotel? Would that really bring in more money?" I asked.

"Considering its location, indeed it would. Some improvements may be in order, but once done, there is no limit to what you could charge for hotel rooms in Baker Street. And referring to your accounts, I see that you have more than adequate means to make such improvements."

"But would that not mean evicting my tenant?" I asked, tentatively.

"It would all be profitable in the long run," said Mr. Greengrass. "It is the most economically sound move that you can make right now."

"Well, I don't know if I could kick out Mr. Holmes," I said, uncertainly. "He has been my tenant for twenty-two years."

"It is your decision," said Mr. Greengrass. "I can only advise what is best for you."

"Well, I shall seriously consider it," I said. "I have to

admit, I see the wisdom in what you say. Baker Street is starting to become very fashionable."

"As for your other accounts," went on Mr. Greengrass. "You have money sitting there which could be invested in the stock market. I am not referring to speculative investing; a wide spread of shares would be essential ..."

"Good gracious, dear me, no," I said. "I would not touch the stock market with a ten foot pole. Property is the only sound investment, as far as I am concerned."

"Very well," said Mr. Greengrass. "Your cash is earning interest at a rate of five per cent per annum. Let us hope that inflation will not get out of control." He closed the file that lay in front of him. "I wish you the very best of luck, Mrs. Hudson," he said, getting up and showing me the door.

As I walked out of the bank, I could not help but notice how the streets of London had changed over the last two decades. A motor car veered dangerously close to the pavement as I walked along Marylebone Road towards my houses in Baker Street. They were adjacent to each other and numbered 221A and 221B. 221A was perfectly sound but I had always preferred 221B. The latter was a self-contained residence with rooms available to let, providing a convenient income. I had done all the required work myself without reliance on a housemaid of any description. My tenants had come and gone, until Mr. Holmes had showed up. At that time, he was not well off, and was obliged to share with an army doctor. I have to admit, when he first moved in, I had had reservations. So undesirable to a landlady were his habits that I had even considered kicking him out; thank goodness I didn't.

I can well remember those first weeks when Mr. Holmes and Dr. Watson moved in. In those days, a housekeeper that I knew by name of Mrs. Turner used to come round regularly. It was early one evening when we were sitting in the front room, partaking of tea, that Mrs. Turner began putting forward some rather adventurous suggestions.

"How are you getting on with your new tenants, —?" she asked. (I shall not reveal my first name, for I prefer to be known respectfully as Mrs. Hudson.)

"Well, they are not quite what I expected," I said, as I poured tea for Mrs. Turner, known to me as Violet. "Eccentric, if you know what I mean. Leastways, Holmes is. Watson is fairly normal and no trouble at all. But Holmes ..."

"What's wrong with him?"

"Well," I said. "For one thing, he is extremely untidy. He can't tidy. What's more, he will not let me near his room, so it is getting gradually into more and more of a mess. I managed to get into the sitting room yesterday, and do you know what I found? The letters V R shot into the wall in a pattern of holes. He is obviously practicing on the premises with his revolver. He has set up some kind of laboratory in one corner of the sitting room, with test tubes and chemicals; not an encouraging sight."

"He sounds like a landlady's worst nightmare," said Mrs. Turner.

"He is. And there's more. When he said he wanted to move in, he did not tell me that he was planning to run a business on the premises."

"That's against your rules, isn't it?" said Mrs. Turner.

"It most certainly is. This business of his involves a lot

of people coming and going on my property. Can you imagine, complete strangers wandering in, expecting me to show them into Holmes' 'consulting room', as he calls it. Though what they are coming to him to consult him about, I can't imagine. They usually stay about half-an-hour or so, then they leave. Presumably they give him money. I should be seeing some of that money."

"You certainly should," said Mrs. Turner. "Either that or inform him that he may not conduct his business in your sitting-room."

"He would not, unfortunately, agree to either," I said. "He doesn't even regard me as the landlady; some kind of housekeeper, that's how he sees me."

"Well, I'm a housekeeper and not ashamed of it," said Mrs. Turner.

"Nor should you be," said I. "But the fact remains that this is my house and he is treating it as though he were its owner."

Mrs. Turner meticulously put down her porcelain cup upon the saucer. "You could always put the rent up," she said.

"Put the rent up? But they've only just moved in."

"How much have they paid in advance?"

"Two weeks," said I. "And two weeks' deposit."

"And do they seem comfortable with the rent that they are paying?"

"Yes," I said. "Very comfortable, I would say. If they each had to foot the bill on their own, I doubt if they could pay, but together, they seem to be breezing it."

"Well, then, they can afford an increase. If they don't want to pay, they can leave. Either way, you win."

"Well, I don't know," I said, hesitatingly. "It seems

rather bad form to put the rent up only two weeks after they have moved in."

"Well, after what you have told me about … what was his name?"

"Sherlock Holmes."

"After what you have told me about Sherlock Holmes, I would have thought you well justified in putting the rent up by twenty-five per cent," said Mrs. Turner. "That's my opinion, anyway."

"Well, I don't think I can go on as it is," I said, slowly. "There are so many things to tolerate. I could tolerate them, I think, if the reward were greater."

"Well, there you are, then," said Mrs. Turner. She looked at her watch. "I must be getting back soon. The master will be wanting his supper. He always has his supper at eight o'clock on the dot. If it's not ready at that time, he goes into a mood."

"Well, at least you know when to cook. Holmes is forever changing the mealtimes. Yesterday he rang for dinner at six, but when I brought it up, he said he would have to turn dinner into supper, for he was going out. He seems to think that meals keep for two hours."

"Just you take my advice," said Mrs. Turner, standing up and getting her hat and coat. "I wouldn't hesitate."

"I'm sure you wouldn't," said I, sincerely. Mrs. Turner was a practical woman. She always came to conclusions far faster than I ever did – no doubt I would have formed exactly the same line of reasoning eventually, had I been left to my own devices. It would have just taken another six months.

I let Mrs. Turner out of the front door. "See you next Thursday, then," she said, waving to me as she hurried off down the street. We always met at the Aerated Bread Company on Thursdays at eleven. I closed the door and went down into the kitchen, which lies at the front of the basement, behind the safety of some iron bars across the windows. I always had to have something ready, in the unlikely event that Holmes was hungry. No doubt Watson would be hungry, but Holmes seemed to be dictating the mealtimes. As I peeled the potatoes, the strains of a violin wafted down from two floors above. Holmes was playing. He never seemed to play any proper pieces; he just tinkered around with notes. On either side of the building were offices, vacant during the evening, so I had told Holmes that he could play then, but not during the day. Much to my relief, he had appeared to understand this.

After a while, I began to muse over what Mrs. Turner had said. How many landladies would put up with a tenant like Holmes? Not very many. He had already broken every rule in the book. Yet did I have the heart to kick him out? It did seem rather unfriendly. And he was certainly very unusual. Not like my previous tenant, Mr. Webster, a clerk who worked in the vicinity and had nothing to say other than repeating whatever was in the newspaper. Sherlock Holmes was in no way describable as boring. No, far better to put the rent up. Mrs. Turner was right in saying that they could both easily afford a bit more. A landlady begins to develop a feel for these things after she has been in the business for a little while. My mind was pretty well made up. The rent was due the following day, so I would tell them that an increase was in order. They could make of that what they liked. Take it or leave it. I suspected that they would take it.

About an hour later the bell from upstairs rang. It appeared that Holmes would be dining in. He was not exactly eating me out of the house; I did have to say that for him. But he did seem awfully pale and thin. I had given up preparing a full English breakfast for him, for he would only partake of a few morsels of it. Breakfast is my strongest meal and my culinary skills in that direction, it would appear, were wasted.

I placed the good, plain fare upon a silver platter and covered it with a silver lid. As I always did, I carried the tray up to the first floor and walked into the room that served as my tenants' sitting room. Holmes was seated at his laboratory; however, on seeing me enter, he immediately put down the test-tube that he was holding and came over to the dining table where Watson was standing.

"Ah, Mrs. Hudson," he said. "I believe you have something important to say to me."

I started. I knew that Holmes was remarkably quick of mind but I had never taken him to be clairvoyant as well.

"Well, yes, Mr. Holmes, I do," I said, recovering myself. "I've been thinking, what with income tax going up and repairs needing doing to the house, I really need to charge you a bit more. From tomorrow, the rent will be six guineas a week."

The two gentlemen who stood at the table looked at me with an expression of horror.

"Six guineas a week?" repeated Dr. Watson. "But we've only been here two weeks."

"Yes, I know, but there it is," I said, observing a burn mark in the carpet.

"Can we manage that, Watson?" said Holmes, turning to the other.

"Well, I suppose I could," said the good doctor. "As long as it doesn't go any higher."

"Yes, all right, then, Mrs. Hudson, you can have your six guineas a week," said Holmes, who appeared to want to forget the subject of money. I immediately departed from the room, quite pleased with myself.

Yes, I can well remember those early days. The first time that I had put up the rent it had felt a bit awkward, but it soon became second nature to me. It was the year 1881 when Holmes moved in and by 1890, he was paying rather more than the going rate. I had raised the rent no less than six or seven times. Holmes had conceded without great hesitation. He seemed to have my welfare at heart. I had finally got used to his disorderly nature, despite the fact that it had worsened since Watson had moved out. Unlike Holmes, by this time the good doctor was now married, although he did drop in from time to time. I remember it was in the afternoon at one such time that I saw him through the kitchen windows, arriving on the doorstep. Mrs. Turner was there; she sometimes filled in for me when I had other business to attend to. I had to go out for an hour. I prepared some cold beef before I left, so it would simply be a matter of taking up the tray for them. When I returned from my errand, Mrs. Turner had put the kettle on and was sitting at the table with the teapot and tea things beside her.

"I hope you don't mind me making myself at home," she said. "I took the tray up, like you said. Gave them a glass of beer as well."

"That's good," I said. "They seem to like simple, plain fare."

I sat down and Mrs. Turner poured me a cup. "You

know," she said. "Judging from that visitor they had yesterday, I would say there was money in the pipeline."

"Whatever do you mean?" I exclaimed.

"Well, I couldn't help noticing that client who came round to see Mr. Holmes last night. I caught a glance of him as he was leaving. I never saw so much silk and astrakhan on one person, and the fur on his boots! He couldn't have been an English gentleman, dressed like that. I reckoned he's a foreign aristocrat and he's being blackmailed. What's more, he's probably paid in advance."

"I never ask Mr. Holmes about his private affairs," I said, stiffly.

"I dare say you don't. But I know an opportunity when I see one. That client is worth something, which means that Holmes is now worth something. Some of it could load off on you if you play your cards right.

"Well, really, Violet," I protested.

"You'll have to find a reason to raise the rent again," said Mrs. Turner. "After this case, I am well sure that he will be able to afford it. As long as you only ever ask him when he can afford it, he should pay up."

"He may not," I objected, drinking my tea. "I have, after all, raised the rent several times already."

"He will have to pay up," said Mrs. Turner. "221B Baker Street has become his official address. That is where he is known to live. He can't change it now."

"I think he would be very reluctant to change it," I said, wondering about this scheme. I remembered the dry rot; that would certainly set me back a pound or two. And it really did seem like Mr. Holmes would be able to afford to pay more money in the very near future, if not already.

"Watson is no longer living here," went on Mrs. Turner. "So you don't have to worry about him objecting. I suggest you confront Holmes at a time when Watson is not present on the premises."

"That is most times," I said. "Why, when he dropped in yesterday, that was the first time that I had seen him in months."

"Oh, well, then it should all be plain sailing."

"You know, I think Mr. Holmes is already rather comfortably off," I said, musingly. "He has had a number of fairly affluent clients. And after this case – who knows? He could even become independent."

"Meaning you could become independent," said Mrs. Turner. "No more carrying trays up and down those stairs."

"You really think the new client is that rich," I said.

"I do. He might even be a prince, for all I know. If Holmes is successful in solving his problems, who knows what reward he will receive: diamonds, jewellery; maybe even a castle, a title or a province in some foreign land."

"I think you are being rather optimistic," I said.

"I am not. I can tell you, this is no ordinary aristocrat. It all depends on how grateful the client is."

"Well, I should think he will be grateful," I said. "The client would not be here unless he had some extremely pressing problem that was preoccupying him. And if he is foreign, as you say, that means he has gone to considerable trouble to get here."

"Well, there you are, then," said Mrs. Turner.

I began to wonder if Mrs. Turner did not have a point. There were repairs to be done to the house and bills have a habit of creeping up on one. It was true that I was not badly off but it does not do to be complacent. Many a well-positioned individual had become poor merely as a result of not keeping track of their finances. It was likely that Holmes would soon be a very wealthy man and would not miss an extra pound a week. Better, however, to wait until the client had paid up and left.

I believe I have been given a present only on two occasions: the first I prefer not to discuss; the second was from Mr. Holmes. The event occurred shortly after the 'foreign aristocrat' had left the country. It appeared that Violet had been correct, as always. In fact, she had underestimated the situation, which was very unusual for her. The foreign aristocrat who had come to see Holmes had been far more than a prince; he was a king. It was shortly after the visitor quitted my premises for the last time that Holmes presented me with a bejewelled box.

"I have been rewarded more than amply for my services in a recent case," he said. "And have no immediate need for this little box. I know that times can be hard for an unprotected woman such as you. I hope that this will add some security to your life."

"Mr. Holmes, your generosity knows no bounds," I said, overwhelmed. I had no intention of refusing the gift but did not wish to seem avaricious. However, it did not seem like a good idea to push my luck. "It really is very good of you, Mr. Holmes," I concluded. "Now I shall be able to see to everything that needs doing in the house." There was plenty that needed doing at 221B, but I had my sights on the house next door, which by some lucky chance, was up for sale. A superficial glance at the box was enough to tell me that it would put down a deposit on that house. I did not hesitate in putting in an offer.

It was a fairly low offer and was initially refused, but the seller came down to it after a while. The premises were set up for office use and when I had bought it I decided to leave it as such, for the prospect of carrying trays around twice as often did not appeal to me. Holmes was barely aware that I had purchased this new set of premises, so wrapped up was he in his own affairs. I did not realize how fraught with danger was his situation at the time; he seemed unduly nervous, but it was not until much later that I realized that this was not without good reason. In April 1891 he disappeared, and did not return. I could not believe the terrible news that he would never be coming back. For a fortnight, his rooms stood empty; I then took the step of re-advertising them, along with the office on the ground floor of 221A, which had recently become vacant. It seemed like no sooner had I placed the advertisements that a respectable-looking young gentleman appeared on my doorstep holding a copy of the newspaper in which the advertisements had appeared. He was of a pristine appearance, and had a smooth, affable sort of manner and an alert expression.

"Good day, Mrs. Hudson," he said, raising his hat. "I have come about the office to let."

"Oh, indeed; well, just let me get the keys and I will show it to you," I said. I opened the door to 221A and showed the gentlemen into the roomy office that led off from the hall, furnished with a desk, chairs and bookshelves. It appeared to be immediately to his liking. "When can I move in?" was his only question.

"Well, as soon as you like," I said. "It is in a state of readiness, as you see."

"Then I should like to move in tomorrow, if that is all

right with you," said the gentleman, who had not as yet told me his name. I went to get the paperwork and we sat at the desk in the office, filling in the details. His name, it turned out, was John Smith.

"Well, I shall look forward to seeing you tomorrow," I said, as he left; as he walked swiftly off down the street I could not help but marvel at the efficiency of the transaction. He had paid me two weeks in advance, so all was currently well. But Holmes' rooms remained empty; that was until a few days later. It was in the late morning that the bell rang out; a tall stout man was at the door. When I opened it, he informed me most cordially that he was Sherlock Holmes' brother.

"I hope you have not yet let the rooms again," said he. "For sentimental reasons I should like to keep them on, although I shall not be living in them, nor shall anybody else. What do you charge?"

"Well, I agreed to let them to another gentleman only a couple of days ago," I said, thoughtfully. "But as he has not returned, I am free to do as I like. As for charges, Mr. Holmes was paying twenty guineas a week before he left us so tragically."

"Twenty guineas a week? That is daylight robbery, Madam. I cannot possibly pay you that. I can't imagine what my brother was thinking of if that was the amount of money he paid to live here. He could have afforded a room at Claridge's for that."

"I dare say," I said, in as offended a tone as I could muster. "However, that is what he was paying."

"I will pay you five guineas a week, and no more," said Mr. Holmes, senior.

I raised myself up to him and said, "There are dozens

of gentlemen in London who would pay that. You are not indispensable, Mr. Holmes." And I made as to shut the door.

"Very well, then," Mr. Holmes. "I will pay the amount you ask. However, I shall not be requiring meals or service of any kind. Presumably that would result in a reduction."

"Yes," I said. "I shall deduct board."

Mr. Holmes produced five ten pound notes. "Here is two weeks in advance," said he. I took the notes without hesitation. It appeared that Holmes was still making me rich, even after his tragic demise. It was a lucky day when he first entered my premises.

Mr. Holmes raised his hat to me and duly left. I placed the notes in a cashbox, locked it and put the box in a drawer in the back room, which I also locked. Then I went to collect a rag and some polish. Even in my new-found state of affluence, I could not bring myself to appoint a slavey. It does not do to start throwing money around, just because it seems like there is some to spare. I took the box outside and began to polish the door furniture of 221B. It was then that I noticed that there was now a sign up beside 221A. I had not given the gentleman to whom I had let the ground floor office permission to put up a sign, but then, it was quite reasonable for him to do so. The lettering upon the sign, however, was not reasonable, for it read:

Sherlock Holmes
Consulting Detective
Appointments not necessary

Never in my born days had I witnessed such brazen effrontery. Poor Mr. Holmes had not been gone three weeks and already, someone was trying to profit from him. I would have stepped into the office right there and then to give him a piece of my mind, but the 'detective' appeared to be away from the premises. I went on polishing the door furniture of both houses and when this was done, went back inside 221B. I then got my hat and coat and went out to meet Mrs. Turner at the Aerated Bread Company.

It was lunchtime and very crowded in the A.B.C. which stood not two hundred yards from my own premises. Mrs. Turner was in there at one of the marble-topped tables in the middle of the hall. She had already ordered a bread roll and coffee. I sat down opposite her and placed my handbag beside me.

"You will not believe what I have just seen," I said, before Mrs. Turner could speak. "You remember that young man to whom I let the office on the ground floor of 221A? Well, it appears that he has set up to impersonate Mr. Holmes."

"Impersonate? How can he do that? I thought that Mr. Holmes was ..."

"He is. But not very many people know that. There was only a brief mention of his departure in a few publications. Most will think he is alive and well."

"Well, that is very likely true," said Mrs. Turner. "But in what way is he impersonating Mr. Holmes?"

"He has put a sign up outside his office to that effect," I said. "I don't know if it is even legal. It does say 221A rather than 221B, but people will find him there all the same. It's quite disgraceful."

"I'd say it was enterprising," said Mrs. Turner.

"You would," I said.

One of the waitresses appeared. "I'll have a cup of tea and a bread roll," I said. "In any case, I intend to kick out this 'gentleman' by the end of the week. I owe it to Mr. Holmes. He has, after all, paid me a princely sum over the years. And I became quite fond of him."

"Perhaps this gentleman will also pay you a princely sum," said Mrs. Turner. "If his business starts to go well. He cannot after all set up as Sherlock Holmes at any other address."

"I do not think that it will go well," I said. "Mr. Holmes had a brain the size of a small planet. This gentleman, whom I have met, did not appear to be any more mentally agile than myself."

"Well, he has Mr. Holmes' reputation," said Mrs. Turner. "That in itself might see him through. Give him a few weeks and see how he gets on."

I was not feeling quite so angry now. Perhaps Mrs. Turner was right. I would be well justified in charging the gentleman an extortionate rent for his blackguard business. Perhaps it was better to let things lie.

When I arrived back the detective was in. What was more, he appeared to have a client, for through the window, I could see a young lady seated opposite him. The detective appeared to be taking notes. I went into 221B. Mr. Mycroft Holmes had instructed me to leave everything in Holmes' rooms exactly as it was, so I never did more than sweep the rugs and some superficial dusting. As I mopped the windows, I observed the young lady who had visited the detective emerge from 221A and walk off down the street. Placing the mop aside, I went back downstairs, with the intention of confronting the new office tenant.

Through the window of 221A, it was apparent that John Smith, or Mr. Sherlock Holmes, was seated at his desk, writing out something. I entered the premises and knocked on the door of the office. "Enter," called out a voice.

"Ah, Mrs. Hudson," said the tenant, as I came in. "What can I do for you?"

"I have observed that you have put up a sign outside the door without my permission," said I. "However, it is not that which concerns me; it is the name upon it. I am quite sure that what you are doing is highly illegal."

"And I am quite sure that it is not," said the tenant. "I changed my name by deed poll to Sherlock Holmes not two days ago. Anyone can set up as a private detective, and anyone can change their name if they so wish."

"Well, really," said I. "Some people have no respect."

The tenant laughed derisively.

"If you wish to operate from these premises," I continued, "You will have to pay a bit more. These are no ordinary premises; they are Sherlock Holmes' premises, at least the rooms next door were. If you insist on using them in this manner, I shall have to double the rent."

"There is a word for this kind of thing," said the tenant. "Opportunism, I believe that it is called."

"Well, you would know," I said. "From a fortnight today, the rent is five guineas a week. You can take it or leave it."

"If you think that I am paying you another penny for your modest premises, you are quite mistaken," said the man. "There is no sane person in London who will pay you that."

"No," I said. "And you will not get far in this business at any other address. On reflection, I have decided that the rent will increase to six guineas a week."

The man put down his pen. "If I were to pay you that," he said, "The rent would increase again in no short space of time, would it not?"

"I never charge more than a tenant can afford," I replied. "In view of the business that you are practising you should think yourself lucky not to be kicked out."

"I will pay you four guineas a week and no more," said the man.

"Make that seven," I said. "Would you like it to be eight?"

The man stared at me contemptuously. "Five it is, then," he said. "I can pay no more."

"That depends upon the quality of your clients," I commented. "We shall review the situation at a later date." Not wishing to spend another minute in the company of so objectionable a man, I left the office and retreated back into my rooms at 221B. I could not imagine that it would be six weeks before his ruse was discovered.

After that event, my remembrance of the years without Holmes is somewhat hazy. Clients continued to turn up at 221B asking for Sherlock Holmes and I had to tell them that he was no longer available. I could not bring myself to tell them what had happened. Soon, even his impersonator was not there to provide them with any kind of solace. But later, the memories become clear again. I shall never forget that April afternoon when Mr. Holmes appeared outside 221B. I was, as you may understand, not expecting it, and became quite hysterical, or so Mr. Holmes told me. He managed to calm me down sufficiently to let him into the premises, after which I informed him that his brother Mycroft had kept the rooms just as he had left them, or thereabouts. It was true that they were tidier than usual, but he was most gratified to find that all his papers were left intact.

"Mrs. Hudson, everything is just as it was before," he exclaimed, as we stood in the sitting room. Mr. Holmes reached for the Persian slipper that lay beside the fireplace and filled his pipe. There was a box of matches on the mantelpiece and he proceeded to light up. He then puffed away nonchalantly, as though the last three years had never happened. But he looked thinner and paler than ever before.

"Would you like some lunch, Mr. Holmes?" I enquired, when I had finally regained my composure.

"I have to say that I would," said Holmes, as he sat down in his old armchair opposite the one that used to be occupied by Dr. Watson. He glanced at his pocket watch. "It is two o'clock now," he said. "I will have to go out at three."

"I still just cannot believe it," I said, wondering at the sight of him. "No wonder your brother wanted to keep on your rooms. I should have guessed." And I left the sitting room, my head still in a whirl, and went down to the kitchen.

When I brought the tray up and entered the sitting room again, Holmes was standing near the window, in the still and contemplative state that he often used to adopt. However, he did not seem to respond to my entrance.

"Mr. Holmes," I said, tentatively. "Your lunch is ready." Yet he still did not respond. I went over to him but he did not seem to notice me. When I touched his arm, I started, for it did not feel human. Then the door to one of the bedrooms opened.

"It's all right, Mrs. Hudson," said Holmes, standing at the threshold. "Life-like, isn't it? I had it made by a craftsman in Grenoble. It is a bust in wax. I have clad it in my best dressing-gown and all it needs now is someone to move it from time to time."

"Why does it need to be moved?" I asked, in awe of the figure that I had genuinely mistaken for my long lost tenant.

"Because, Mrs. Hudson, if it does not occasionally move, it will eventually become obvious to anyone observing it that it is not real. I regret to inform you that this house is being watched."

"Good Heavens, Mr. Holmes," I said. "Is somebody after you?"

"Most definitely," said Holmes. "And tonight is the one and only opportunity to confront the danger that I, and possibly you too, Mrs. Hudson, are in. If all goes well, I shall soon overcome the perils that we face. But I need your help."

"Me, Mr. Holmes?"

"Yes, you. You are in fact the only person who can help me. If you do, I shall reward you handsomely, for I am not without means."

"What do you want me to do?" I asked, at once.

"I need you to get down on your knees and move the bust to a different position once every fifteen minutes or thereabouts, so as to give the impression to anyone who is watching it from outside the house that it is a living thing. But keep down. Should a bullet come through the window, it will most likely go through the head of the bust."

"I should think I could do that," I said. It was not the first time that Holmes had brought danger to the household. "Then I shall feel that I am in safe hands," said Holmes, disappearing back into the bedroom again. I left the tray on the table and went back downstairs. Half-an-hour later, an elderly, deformed man with sharp, wizened features and white hair came down the stairs. I was quite sure that no such person had entered, but was not alarmed for I was quite accustomed to Holmes and his bizarre disguises. He nodded to me as he passed me in the hallway and left the house.

Well, I was still in quite a tense state, what with the day's events and the evening to come. Holmes had mentioned something about bullets, meaning that someone wanted to kill him. I looked out into the street from the front room but could see nobody loitering. Perhaps they were watching from one of the houses on the opposite side of the road. Then I realized that the tramp who was standing by the lamppost could certainly be the one. I was about to go out and question him but then decided that Mr. Holmes would not want me to do that.

At six o'clock I went upstairs and moved the bust to a place visible through the window, as arranged. I was down on my knees and kept to the front of it, so that my shadow might not be seen. The bust was currently providing a side view to anyone who might be watching. I could not help marvelling at how exactly like Mr. Holmes it was. Not even at Madame Tussauds would you have found such detailed specimens. I then crept out of the room, again on my hands and knees. Fifteen minutes later I returned, dutifully repeating the process. Where was Holmes? I hoped sincerely that nothing had or was going to happen to him. When I entered the room on my knees for the third time, I came across what looked extremely like a bullet, lying on the floor. The bust was still standing; however, I could not stand up to examine whether the bullet had gone through it. Instead, I picked up the bullet and left the room. It would not do to move the bust if Holmes was supposed to have been shot.

I remember very well that I felt more than relieved when Holmes appeared much later that evening, right as rain, accompanied by Dr. Watson, who looked as sanguine as ever.

"I hope you observed all precautions, Mrs. Hudson?" said Holmes.

"I went to it on my knees, sir, just as you told me," I said.

"Excellent. You carried the thing out very well. Did you observe where the bullet went?"

"Yes, sir," I said. "I'm afraid it has spoilt your beautiful bust, for it passed right through the head and flattened itself on the wall. I picked it up from the carpet. Here it is!"

Holmes held it out to Dr. Watson. "A soft revolver bullet, as you perceive, Watson. There's genius in that, for who would expect to find such a thing fired from an airgun? All right, Mrs. Hudson." He dismissed me in his usual manner. I left the room with confidence that I would be duly rewarded for my services in the not too distant future.

With these reminiscences I reached Baker Street and went on up to my houses. Should they be turned into an hotel, they would have to be merged. They would then become 221 Baker Street, a far more auspicious address. That was in fact how the building had been in Georgian times, when people were richer. Only later had it been split into two houses. It seemed fitting to restore the building to its former glory. The only problem was Mr. Holmes. As I opened the door, I could hear his violin coming from upstairs. He still seemed to feel very much at home here. But my mind was made up.

I placed my handbag upon the side-table, removed my hat and coat, and went upstairs. For what must have been the first time ever, I knocked.

"Come in, Mrs. Hudson," called out Mr. Holmes' familiar, affable voice. I did so, and he stood before me apprehensively, holding his violin. This he placed in its case, which lay on the table nearby. "I take it you have some bad news for me," he said.

Mr. Holmes was always making statements of this kind, and just for once, I asked him how he knew.

"When you entered the room, you were not carrying a tray or scuttle, and a brief glance out of the window earlier told me that no one was at the door. You are not prone to social calls," he said. "I therefore assumed that you had come up here because you had something to tell me. In addition to this, your tread upon the stairs was slower than usual, indicating that you were not looking forward to the task ahead. A faster tread would have indicated good news. When you arrived at the door, you knocked, a most unusual if not unique, occurrence, indicating that what you had to say might offend me, and wished to pre-empt it with politeness."

"Well, Mr. Holmes," I said. "I wonder why you don't

go into the fortune-telling business. All you need is a bandana and a crystal ball, and you would be away."

"You could be right," said Mr. Holmes. "It is a mistake for me to explain my methods. Far better merely to state the result without giving the cause. A career in fortune-telling might be the very thing, for I am in fact looking for a change in profession."

"You are?" I gasped in amazement.

Mr. Holmes went over to the writing table and picked up a photograph that lay there. He showed it to me, with great enthusiasm. It was a picture of a villa situated upon a slope that led down to a coast-line of white cliffs.

"As you can probably guess, the house is situated on the southern coast of England. It lies in the Sussex Downs, five miles from Eastbourne."

"What about your clients?" I asked. "They won't want to trek all the way down there."

"There will be no clients," said Mr. Holmes. "I shall retire. And now for your news," he said, with a change in his tone of voice. "Let me hear the worst of it."

"Well, if you are leaving of your own accord, it is of no importance," I said. "However, honesty compels me to tell you what I came here to say. I am turning this house and the one next door into an hotel."

"What a marvellous idea, Mrs. Hudson," said Holmes. "I can't think why you did not do so before."

"You will never be forgotten, Mr. Holmes," I said. "I shall put up a sign above this door, to indicate that you graced these very rooms with your presence. I shall call them, 'The Sherlock Suite'."

"And charge fifty guineas a night, no doubt" said Mr. Holmes. "You have done well out of me over the years;

I must have paid you the price of this house three times over in rent."

"You should have bought yourself, Mr. Holmes," I said.

"And so I shall," said he, picking up the photograph again. "This villa lies on a bee-farm. I intend to buy the estate."

"A bee-farm!" I exclaimed, in disbelief. "What on earth do you want with bees?"

"The beehive is a most ingenious marvel of nature," said Mr. Holmes. "Within it lies a whole society, not unlike our own. I intend to study the art of bee-keeping, amongst other things."

"Well, each to his own," I said. It was only to be expected that Mr. Holmes would come up with an eccentric idea like this.

"I shall be needing a housekeeper," went on Mr. Holmes. "I don't suppose that you would ..."

"No, I would not," I said, indignantly. "It may have escaped your notice, but I am in fact the landlady of this establishment and not the housekeeper."

"No matter," said Mr. Holmes. "I let it slip that I was thinking of retiring to the Sussex Downs to keep bees and this has prompted a stream of letters from women who wish to take on the position. One even says that she is an expert at segregating the queen, and that she is therefore predestined to become my housekeeper."

"Indeed," I said. "Well, Mr. Holmes, I am sure you know what you are doing. I expect you will get tied up in new cases wherever you are."

"That may be so," said Holmes. "However, I have no such intentions at present."

"I see you have already started packing," I said, noting the box, previously stacked on top of the wardrobe, now lying open in one corner of the room.

"Yes," said Holmes. "That is the same trunk with which I arrived, all those years ago. You know, it seems like yesterday that I first entered these rooms. I took to them immediately and was then granted a second stroke of luck upon meeting Dr. Watson the next day. I only regret that Watson has deserted me for a wife once more. I doubt if I shall be seeing him with any kind of frequency."

"I hope you will not be too lonely down in Eastbourne," I said. But I knew he wouldn't be; there would be cases to solve, whether he like it or not, and he would no doubt summon his friend to assist.

"Will you be staying here after the house has been converted into an hotel?" enquired Holmes, as he began to pile up some of his books.

"Oh, no," I said. "I shall return to my native Scotland, a place that I have begun to miss in the last few years." Holmes now seemed rather busy so I left him to attend to his affairs.

In the comfort of my chamber I sat down at my writing desk. I unlocked the uppermost drawer and took out a large envelope: from it, I drew out the deeds to a castle situated in Dunbartonshire, close to the village of Arrochar; it would be my future home. Its towers, turrets and moat were all I could wish for. Throughout my entire life, I have rarely missed an opportunity nor wasted a penny. As a result, I am now, I believe, one of the upper million. It just shows what can be done in time with a little thought.